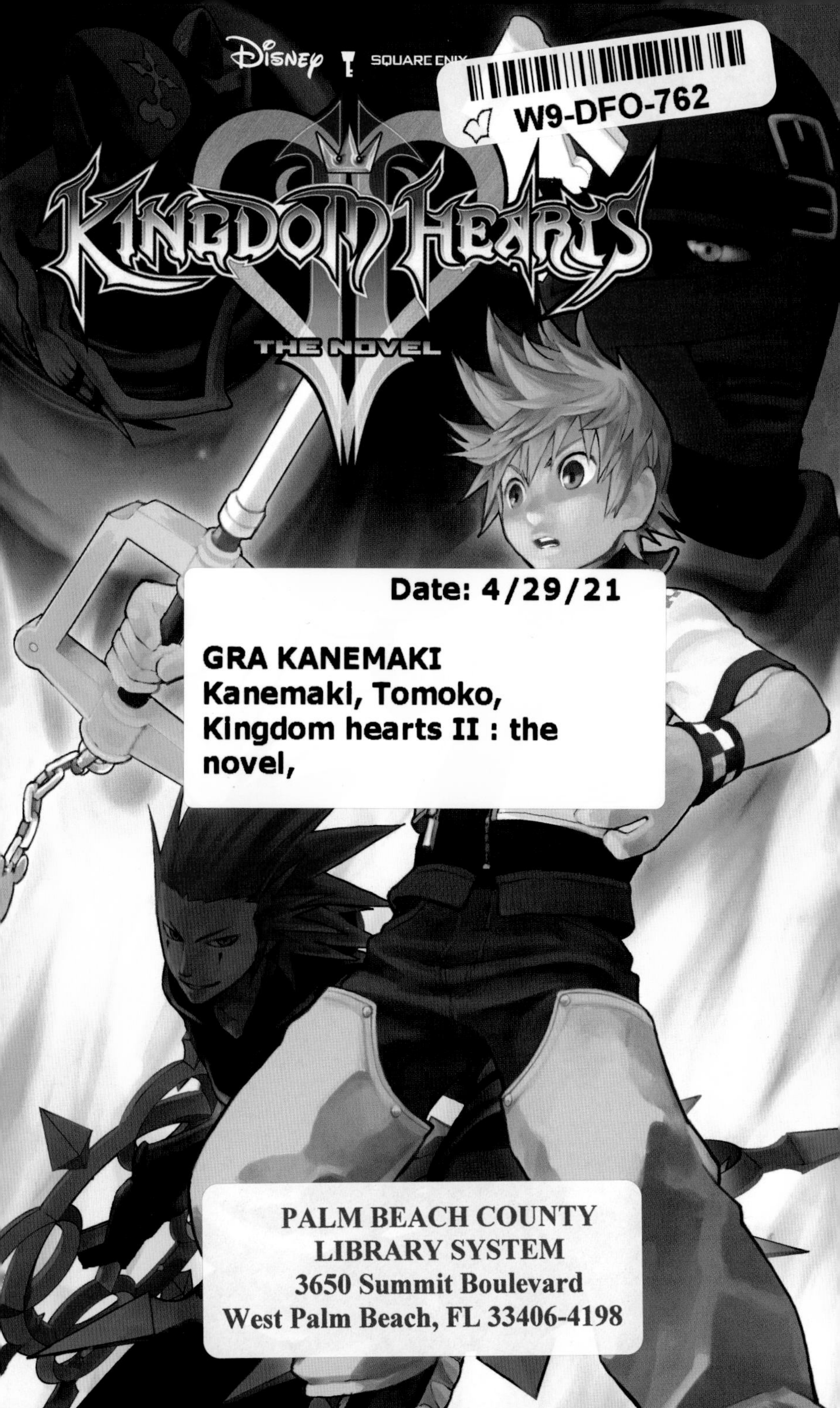
Disney
SQUARE ENIX
Kingdom Hearts II
THE NOVEL

Vol. 1

Tomoco Kanemaki

Original Concept
Tetsuya Nomura
Kazushige Nojima

Illustrations
Shiro Amano

KINGDOM HEARTS II: THE NOVEL, Vol. 1
TOMOCO KANEMAKI,
ILLUSTRATIONS: SHIRO AMANO,
ORIGINAL CONCEPT: TETSUYA NOMURA, KAZUSHIGE NOJIMA

Translation by Melissa Tanaka
Cover art by Shiro Amano

Yen On
1290 Avenue of the Americas
New York, NY 10104

Visit us at yenpress.com
facebook.com/yenpress
twitter.com/yenpress
yenpress.tumblr.com
instagram.com/yenpress

First Yen On Edition: June 2017

Yen On is an imprint of Yen Press, LLC.
The Yen On name and logo are trademarks of Yen Press, LLC.

The publisher is not responsible for websites (or their content) that are not owned by the publisher.

Library of Congress Cataloging-in-Publication Data
Names: Kanemaki, Tomoko, 1975– author. | Amano, Shiro, illustrator. | Tanaka, Melissa, translator.
Title: Kingdom hearts II : the novel / Tomoco Kanemaki ; illustrations, Shiro Amano ; translation by Melissa Tanaka.
Description: First Yen On edition. | New York, NY : Yen On, 2017–
Identifiers: LCCN 2017016091 | ISBN 9780316471930 (v. 1 : paperback)
Subjects: | CYAC: Fantasy. | Friendship—Fiction. | BISAC: JUVENILE FICTION / Fantasy & Magic. | JUVENILE FICTION / Media Tie-In.
Classification: LCC PZ7.1.K256 Ki 2017 | DDC [Fic]—dc23
LC record available at https://lccn.loc.gov/2017016091

ISBNs: 978-0-316-47193-0 (paperback)
978-0-316-55960-7 (ebook)

3 5 7 9 10 8 6 4

LSC-C

Printed in the United States of America

Vol. 1

ROXAS — SEVEN DAYS

CONTENTS

THE DESTRUCTION OF HOLLOW BASTION

CONTENTS

THE MAN IN THE BLACK CLOAK
A mysterious figure working with DiZ and Naminé who makes contact with Roxas. He always wears his hood pulled down over his face—as if he's trying to hide it.
DIZ
A strange man who wears red bandages over his face and a red cape. He's observing Roxas's every move, but why is a mystery. He appears to know King Mickey.
KING MICKEY
The king of Disney Castle. Like Sora, he has a Keyblade and travels around to save worlds. He fought alongside Riku in Castle Oblivion.
NAMINÉ
A girl with the power to unchain people's memories and link them back together in different ways. She was imprisoned in Castle Oblivion by Organization XIII.
AXEL
Number 8 of Organization XIII and the only surviving member who was at Castle Oblivion. He's trying to get Roxas to remember something...

SORA
A fifteen-year-old boy and the wielder of the Keyblade. Cheerful and straightforward, he has a strong sense of right and wrong. Along with Donald and Goofy, he was on a journey searching for Kairi and Riku. To restore the memories he lost, Sora fell into a deep sleep in Castle Oblivion.
ROXAS
A boy who lives in Twilight Town and a pretty good skateboarder. He finds his very normal life interrupted by dreams about Sora, a boy he's never even met. And then things begin to get weird in real life, too.
PENCE
HAYNER
OLETTE
Friends of Roxas in Twilight Town. Their ringleader is Hayner, a boy with an "attitude." Olette, the mature one, keeps everyone in line, while Pence is carefree but clever. During summer vacation, they can always be found hanging out at their usual spot.

MALEFICENT
She failed in her attempt to open the door to darkness and control the Heartless. Sora and his friends defeated her, but she's recovered and is determined to conquer the worlds this time.
PETE
He was banished to another dimension for his endless wrongdoing. Maleficent helped him escape, and now he's working with her to take over the worlds.
RIKU (ANSEM)
A sixteen-year-old boy who lived on Destiny Island, where he was Sora's best friend and sometimes a friendly rival. In Castle Oblivion, he chose to fight with the darkness in his heart controlled by Ansem rather than seal his heart away. That decision transformed him—and now he wears Ansem's appearance.
NAMINÉ
A girl with the power to unchain people's memories and link them back together in different ways. Under the orders of the organization in Castle Oblivion, she dismantled Sora's memories.
PLUTO
King Mickey's beloved dog, who can sniff out important things, and important people. He tends to appear at interesting moments.
AXEL
Number 8 of Organization XIII and once a close friend to Roxas. He was trying to get Roxas to remember him but had to fight him on the orders of the organization—and lost.

SORA
A fifteen-year-old boy and the wielder of the Keyblade. Cheerful and straightforward, he has a strong sense of right and wrong. With his friends Donald and Goofy, he's on a quest to find Kairi and Riku. He still doesn't know that Roxas, who was living in Twilight Town, was a piece of himself—his Nobody.
GOOFY
The captain of the knights at Disney Castle. He followed Donald, who left the castle in search of their king. With his laid-back nature, he fights with his shield to knock aside enemies rather than using something pointy like a sword. He's usually easygoing, but his strength and courage will come out in a pinch.
DONALD DUCK
The royal magician of Disney Castle. Obeying a message from King Mickey to follow the Keyblade wielder, he travels the worlds along with Sora. He's stubborn and hotheaded, but trusts his friend Sora and helps along the way with his powerful magic and store of knowledge.
KAIRI
A fifteen-year-old girl and a good friend of Sora and Riku. She has the power to close the door to darkness. Now, she's back on Destiny Island, waiting for her friends to come home.
KING MICKEY
The king of Disney Castle. Like Sora, he has a Keyblade and travels around to save worlds. He fought alongside Riku in Castle Oblivion.

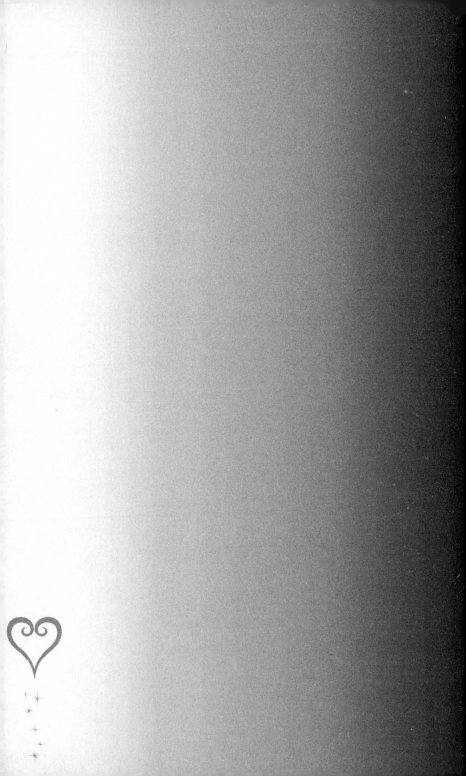

ROXAS—SEVEN DAYS

What's happening to me...?
Falling...falling into darkness.........?

Memories fading.
Memories reborn.
And a dream—
A dream of you,
in a world
without you.

PROLOGUE
EPISODE ONE

AFTER THEY CLOSED THE KEYHOLE, SORA AND HIS friends thought they would find the princesses standing at the door in Hollow Bastion, awaiting their return. But instead they stepped through the door into a strange place shrouded in mist.

"Huh…?" Donald cocked his head.

"Now where are we…?" Sora mumbled, looking around. Then a strange sensation came over him.

"Ah. It seems you are special, too."

At the sudden voice behind him, Sora turned. "Who are you?!"

He saw a man standing there alone, wearing a black cloak, looking down at Sora from beneath a hood.

"Ansem…?" Goofy said uncertainly, and readied his shield behind Sora.

The man seemed like Ansem. But the hood covering his face made it hard to tell who it was. Tensed for a fight, Sora and his friends glared at the mysterious figure.

"That name rings familiar…," the man murmured, as if to himself, and then spoke to Sora again. "You remind me of him."

"What's that supposed to mean?!" Sora shot back, taking a stance with the Keyblade. He had no idea who the man was talking about.

"It means you are not whole. You are incomplete. Allow me…to test your strength."

The man approached, gliding over the floor, and flung orbs of light from his hands. The attack struck Sora and sent him sprawling.

"Sora!" Goofy cried, running to his defense, but the man drew twin swords from his cloak and knocked Goofy back.

"Firaga! Thundaga! Blizzaga!" Donald hurled spells at the man, but they all dissipated harmlessly without even singeing the black cloak.

"...Impressive," said the man. "This will be enjoyable."

"What are you talking about...?!" Sora shouted, springing to his feet.

"It is beyond your comprehension for now. Until we meet again," the man replied softly. The blades disappeared from his hands.

"Wait—who *are* you?!"

"I am...but a mere shell." With that, the man vanished like smoke into the air.

Still clutching the Keyblade, Sora stared in confusion. And then a voice he knew spoke.

"Good work, Sora."

He turned to find Leon standing there. "Are we back...?"

"Something wrong, Sora?" Leon asked, seeing him looking so bewildered.

"No... It's nothing." Sora grinned and ran ahead to the final battle—the fight against Ansem.

When he came to, he was standing somewhere else. It was the edge of the world—or so he felt. Jagged, crumbling rocks jutted up from a dark seashore.

But come to think of it, hadn't he sat in a place sort of like this, talking about the future?

A blue sea...a blue sky...

The scene simply floated up in his mind, and he shook his head. *That couldn't have happened.*

Then he glanced down at himself. He was wearing unfamiliar black clothes—a cloak, to be precise. He knew he was seeing himself for the first time, but strangely, nothing about his appearance seemed wrong.

"So, you've arrived," said a voice behind him.

He turned and saw a figure much like himself—someone wearing a black cloak, face completely hidden under a hood. His own expression was most likely concealed from the other man, too.

"I've been to see him."

Him?

He nearly asked who the other man meant, but he had a vague sense that he already knew. He bit back the question.

"He looks a lot like you."

Right—and I probably look a lot like him. He and I are two sides of the same coin...

"Who are you?" he asked the other man.

"I'm what's left. An empty shell. Or maybe I'm all there ever was."

He frowned slightly at the man's evasive reply. "I meant your name."

Yes—he wanted to know the *name* of the person standing before him.

"My name is of no importance. What about you? Do you remember your true name?"

It sounded almost like the man was taunting him. He opened his mouth to respond...

To say *his* name. The name of the one in the very depths of his memory.

"My true name...is..."

And here...the story begins.

CHAPTER 1
THE 1st DAY

UNDER THE SOFT LIGHT SPILLING IN THROUGH THE window, Roxas slowly opened his eyes.

"Another dream about him...," he mumbled, then stood up on his bed to fling the window wide open. The warm, faintly humid summer air rushed in. His chestnut hair shone honey-gold in the light. From his room on the second floor, Roxas could see a broad swath of the town.

A dream... Ever since the beginning of summer vacation, Roxas had been having the same dreams every night. Dreams of a vivid blue sky over a brilliant sea of the same color, and a boy, named for that sky. The boy's name was...

"......Sora."

Roxas murmured it to himself and blinked his blue eyes.

The boy in the dream, Sora, had a smile as bright as the sky. *He seems nice enough*, Roxas thought. But he couldn't quite say how he felt about the boy.

From a distance he heard the bells ringing. That was the town's distinctive landmark—the clock tower above the station. The two bells that stuck out from it on each side told time for all the citizens of Twilight Town.

Roxas stretched and hopped off his bed. He took off his pajamas—a plain white shirt and capris—and dressed in a white jacket and black pants before leaving his room.

Roxas headed to the usual spot—an old storage space under the train tracks. His friends were already there, Hayner and Pence and Olette, chatting about something.

"Hey, Roxas," Olette said, noticing him.

"Oh—hi." Roxas looked back at his friends, each seated in a corner.

"Roxas, you gotta hear this, too!" Hayner blurted, a bit loud, as usual. He wore pants and shoes with a camouflage pattern and a black T-shirt emblazoned with a skull, and as always, his wavy, light-brown hair was impeccably styled. "Man, doesn't it tick you off?" he said to the others.

"Yeah, that's just wrong," Pence agreed, angrily shaking his head, though his bristly black hair didn't ruffle in the slightest. It looked coarse enough to hurt if it were to fall in his eyes—maybe that was why he wore it bound up in a hair band. He wore an oversize basketball shirt by Dog Street, featuring the brand's logo and stylized dog character chasing bones. It suited his sturdy build perfectly.

"Seifer's gone too far this time," Olette added. Her orange tank top with the four-leaf-clover design at the hip was her favorite shirt. She always regarded everyone with kindness, no matter what. Even Seifer.

"I mean, it's true that stuff's been getting stolen around town. And we've never gotten along with Seifer. So if he wants to think we did it, I can't really blame him. What's really driving me nuts is that he's going around tellin' everybody that we're the thieves! Now the whole town is treating us like a bunch of criminals! Have you ever been this mad in your *life*?" Hayner ranted all in one breath, and jumped down from the wooden crate that made his usual perch, shaking a fist. "'Cos I haven't. Nuh-uh, never. So, what to do…?"

Hayner turned and stared at Roxas, who hadn't quite been listening.

Roxas paused, surprise crossing his face, and then he jumped to his feet. "Um, well… We could find the real thieves. That would set the record straight."

"Hey, that sounds kinda fun," Pence said, getting out of his chair.

Not quite satisfied, Hayner stuck out his lips in a pout. "What about Seifer?"

Beside him, Pence rushed to the box that they called the treasure chest and rummaged through it.

"First, we gotta clear our names," Roxas said. "Once we find the real culprit, everyone will get off our back."

"Oh no!" Pence looked up from the box, holding a compact camera.

"Now what?" Hayner shot Pence a look, offended by the interruption.

"They're gone! Our ——— are gone!"

Roxas, Hayner, and Olette all ran to look in the box.

"What? How? All our ——— are gone?" Olette said, and then touched her throat, looking nervously at Roxas.

Not only were their things gone—the word itself was gone…?

"Stolen…," Roxas said. "Even the word ——— got stolen?"

Hayner nodded and caught his eye. "There's no way Seifer could've done this."

Roxas nodded in reply.

"Okay. Time for some recon!" Hayner dashed out of their hangout. Pence and Olette followed him.

"All right!" Roxas moved to catch up—and the world began spinning. "…Huh?"

The strength drained from his legs, but by the time he realized he was crumpling to the floor, darkness was swallowing his mind.

A deep voice spoke from somewhere.

"His heart is returning. Doubtless he'll awaken very soon."

But…Roxas didn't know who it was.

It's already been one year since I promised him, Naminé thought.

Sora was asleep in the flower-bud capsule. It had been a year since he went in.

She looked away, down at the floor. *Maybe we're just being used.*

"…Naminé."

Slowly she turned to face the person addressing her.

The man wore a black cloak, the same as those in the organization. There was kindness in the eyes that she glimpsed beneath the hood—eyes that could never lie.

She'd spent this past year doing nothing but drawing pictures… but for *him*, it had been a very hard year.

"It won't be much longer." His gaze was fixed on the sleeping Sora.

Everything he *does is for Sora…and for all the worlds. So what about me? What am I doing here?* Naminé asked herself.

"He seems lonely somehow," *he* said.

"I wouldn't worry."

A small smile curled the edges of Naminé's mouth. She returned her attention to Sora.

Soon... Soon, Sora will wake up.

But then what will he do?

And what about us? Do we have to meet the same fate as that false one, the Replica? Is there no other way?

Naminé thought of the chestnut-haired boy who had come into being in the same moment she had.

What...was that voice just now?

Roxas looked around. He knew he'd heard someone speaking. About his heart returning.

"Roxas?" He raised his head to see Pence peering anxiously at him. "C'mon, let's go."

"Yeah..."

Pence grabbed his hand and pulled him to his feet, and they left the space under the tracks. Outside was a sloping back alley, leading up toward the station and down to the sandlot.

"Roxas, what're you doing?!" Hayner shouted from downhill.

If they ran straight ahead, they would come to the tram common at the center of town.

"Hurry up!" Hayner yelled again.

"Okay!" Roxas chased after Pence.

But that voice...where did it come from?

And those dreams...about Sora. What does it all mean?

"Over here!" Hayner called.

Roxas followed his voice through the gate and dashed into the plaza.

The stillness of the room was only broken by a mechanical sound.

The only light in the dim space came from the computer screens. A man headed toward one of them and typed something on the keyboard.

The man's face was wrapped in red cloth bandages and black leather belts. There were things he had to record. The experiments that had led to all this... The root of all these evils was within him.

Little electronic noises broke the room's silence.

"It seems we have some contaminants...," he murmured to himself.

The man's name was DiZ. It stood for "Darkness in Zero."

This was the name he'd chosen for himself—and the burden he'd brought upon himself.

"Time to get this investigation under way!" Pence declared when Roxas caught up. The four of them gathered in the middle of the common to confer.

"Did you find out who's been robbed?" Hayner asked.

"Sure did!" replied Pence. "Wallace at the Item Shop, Jessie at the Accessory Shop, Auntie Elmyra at the Candy Shop...and..."

"That's practically everyone in town who runs a shop!" Olette exclaimed.

"Well, I guess we'll have to go around and ask them one by one," Hayner said with a sigh.

"You're right," Roxas agreed. They headed to the Item Shop.

"Roxas," Wallace started before any of them could get a word in. "Never thought you'd do such a rotten thing..."

"We didn't steal anything, okay?" Roxas said.

Wallace only shook his head. "I'd like to believe you, but...who else would take that stuff?"

"Could you tell us what got stolen?" Olette asked, standing beside Roxas.

"As if you kids didn't already know," Wallace said icily. "Look, I'm not gonna talk to you. Go to the Accessory Shop and ask Jessie."

Apparently there was no doubt in his mind that Roxas and his friends were the thieves.

"What a drag... Well, we better talk to Jessie." Hayner spun on his heels and fixed his sights on the Accessory Shop.

Pence followed suit. "Even if Seifer was spreading rumors about us...didn't Wallace seem a little *too* convinced that we're guilty?"

"Yeah, well, it's Seifer's fault! Why else would everyone think it was us without any evidence?" Hayner said.

Pence and Olette both tilted their heads in thought.

"Hey...are all of us suspects or just me?" Roxas wondered aloud.

"Saying *you* are is the same as saying all of us are!" Hayner clenched his fists.

"But..." Dejected, Roxas lowered his head. *Wallace definitely suspected me and no one else.*

"That's right," Pence said. "Besides, you'd never be able to steal things on your own without getting caught."

"I guess so— Hey! What's that supposed to mean, Pence?"

When Roxas looked up, Pence covered his head against retaliation and sprinted ahead.

"Well, it's true," Olette giggled. "There's just no way you could pull off anything so scandalous." She took off after Pence.

"Aw, c'mon! You too, Olette?!" Roxas complained, and chased after them.

"Hey—wait for me!" Hayner ran to catch up.

The four of them stopped short outside the Accessory Shop.

"Oh, it's you, Roxas..." The voice from behind the counter belonged to the pretty shopkeeper, Jessie. "I wish you wouldn't let me down. You used to be one of my favorite customers."

"I'm not a thief!" Roxas felt like he was repeating himself. It hurt to be presumed guilty like this.

"But there's no one else who would steal those things," Jessie said.

Roxas hung his head.

Hayner spoke up behind him. "Roxas says he didn't do it!"

"Well, it doesn't really matter." Jessie let out a small sigh.

"What got stolen? Can you tell us anything?" Olette asked persistently.

Jessie's shoulders sagged, as if she didn't want to talk about it. "Anyway, you'll have to find a way to clear your name. Elmyra at the Candy Shop is pretty disappointed, too."

"Let's go, Roxas." Pence gently pushed him away from the counter, apparently convinced that there was no point in asking any more questions. The four of them trudged to the Candy Shop.

"I'm *not* a thief...," Roxas mumbled.

"We know that. That's why we're asking around, isn't it? After all, we were robbed, too!" Hayner gave him a friendly thump on the back as they ran up to the counter. "Hey, Auntie!"

Elmyra looked up. "Oh, hello there, Hayner. Sea-salt ice cream for you?" she said in her slow, easygoing way.

"We wanted to ask if anyone stole things from you," Hayner said. The others clustered around him, all of them watching Auntie Elmyra.

"Oh my, yes. Something important," she replied, and the black cat perched on her lap softly meowed.

"Just so you know, we didn't do it," Roxas suddenly declared.

Auntie Elmyra looked squarely back at him. "I believe you," she told him warmly, with a faint smile.

"Thank you, ma'am," Olette said. "So, what did they take from you?"

"I can't say the word, but... My ——. My precious ——." She sounded mournful.

"They took ours, too!" Pence cried.

"So, the culprit is going around stealing ——. And not just ——, but the word ——, too," Hayner said, looking at Roxas.

He nodded. *But why would a thief steal ——?*

"I wonder if Seifer knows anything about it," Olette murmured.

"We'll have to go ask him," Roxas said. The other three nodded. "Thanks, Auntie Elmyra!"

They waved to her and took off for the sandlot.

"Thieves!"

Fuu's voice sounded from the sandlot the moment she saw Roxas and his friends.

"That was real low, y'know!" Rai added.

"Oh yeah?!" Hayner ran straight down to them.

In the sandlot stood Fuu, a slender girl with a piercing gaze who spoke strangely in clipped phrases, and Rai, a brawny boy who had nothing but the greatest respect for Seifer. With them was Vivi, a timid boy who seldom said a word. This trio was Seifer's retinue.

"You better take that back!" Hayner shouted.

He was on the verge of tackling Rai when Seifer strode onto the scene from the path leading to Station Heights. "Nice comeback."

Hayner jumped and spun around. "What'd you say?!"

But Seifer brushed past Hayner to face Roxas. "You can give us back the ——— now."

"I didn't steal it," Roxas said, glaring back.

"You're the only one who would!" Rai retorted from behind his hero.

"It was our proof that we totally whooped your butts," Seifer went on. "So, what'd you do? Burn it? Not like getting rid of it would change the fact that you're losers."

"Rematch!" Fuu declared.

Rai laughed loudly. "Yeah! That'll be rich!"

"If you surrender now, I might just let it slide," Seifer said with a healthy dose of swagger, and he drew the toy sword that was his weapon of choice.

"Roxas…," Olette called nervously.

But Roxas stepped closer and knelt down, then lowered his head.

"Ah-ha-ha! Beggin' for forgiveness?!" Rai taunted.

Instead, Roxas picked up another toy sword from the ground and swung it at Seifer.

"Hey—are you for real?"

"Yeah, I am!"

The two boys battled for a bit until Roxas finally knocked Seifer's sword from his hands. He glared at Seifer as he tried to catch his breath.

Hayner jumped up and cheered. "All right, Roxas!"

As if that took the wind out of his sails, Seifer simply walked away, leaving his sword where it had fallen in the dirt.

"Seifer's just not feelin' so hot, y'know!" said Rai.

"Tournament decides!" Fuu added.

They followed Seifer, and then Vivi toddled away after them.

"Nice work, Roxas!" Pence took the camera from his pocket and aimed it.

"Huh? Oh, okay..." Seeing the lens trained on him, Roxas struck a victorious pose and grinned. The shutter clicked.

And that instant—

Something appeared out of nowhere and swiped Pence's camera.

"Whoa!" Startled, Pence fell backward.

The thing that held his camera was some kind of creature they'd never seen before, gleaming silver and writhing strangely, like a mirage that warped the air around it.

"What's that?!" Hayner yelped as the thing slinked and hopped away toward the alley that led to the plaza below.

"The thief!" cried Olette.

Still clutching the toy sword, Roxas ran after it.

"H-hey, slow down, Roxas!" he heard Hayner call, but he wasn't about to stop.

This is the thief...! Roxas was absolutely certain of it. The weird creature dashed out of the sandlot, then cut across the tram common—it was ridiculously fast. It slithered into a hole in the wall at the edge of the plaza.

"Is it heading for that haunted mansion...?" he muttered as he ducked through the hole into the dim, quiet woods.

In the woods, there was a huge old house where no one lived—haunted, supposedly. The thing seemed to be moving steadily toward the gap in the trees, where Roxas could just barely see the lighter patch ahead.

It stopped in front of the mansion's gate. Roxas lifted his toy sword and crept closer to it.

But the thing suddenly froze still—and at the same time Roxas heard a voice that seemed to speak directly into his body.

"We have come for you, my liege."

"Huh?" Roxas blurted.

The thing rushed at him.

"Augh!" He swung at the winding, writhing creature. He was sure he'd made contact, and yet the sword seemed to go right through it.

"It's no good… Why can't I hit it?"

The moment he lowered his sword, the world went askew.

"Not again…!" It felt like what had happened to him back in the hangout.

But not exactly the same. This time, there was a quiet, electronic kind of sound.

Light gathered around the toy sword in his hand. It looked like there were spirals of numbers swirling around it.

"Huh?"

And before his eyes, the sword transformed—into a giant key.

"What…is this thing?"

The key seemed to draw him forward, moving on its own to attack the creature. "Whoa!"

This time, when the key made contact, Roxas felt the impact. A second and a third strike, and then the strange creature vanished like it had been an illusion the whole time. Likewise, the giant key he held changed back into wood.

He had no idea what was happening.

A giant key…and a strange creature.

Those voices from nowhere…and those dreams.

"Roxas!" That voice was Hayner's.

There on the ground, exactly where the creature had been, were a few pieces of paper. Roxas picked one up. It was a photo of himself with Wallace from the Item Shop.

"Are you okay?!" Pence called out. Olette joined them a moment later.

"Yeah… Look." Roxas held up the picture.

"Are these the ones that got stolen?" Hayner said, peering at it.

"I think so…"

Pence and Olette gathered the other photos.

"Well, looks like this is all the missing stuff," Pence said, picking up his camera.

"Back to our usual spot?" Olette suggested.

"Yeah…" Roxas nodded.

A gathering of men in black cloaks sat in a great hall of shining white marble. Their hoods hid their faces, making their expressions unreadable. There were seven of them, and their seats were according to some kind of numbered order. Six seats were empty—numbers 4 and 5, 6, 11, 12, and 13.

"It seems we've found him at last," the man in seat 1 said in a deep voice.

"Roxas?" asked the man in seat 2. "Or the hero…?"

"Both."

Number 8 looked away from number 1's high seat near him and shrugged.

Another man slowly shook his head. "Both of them at once? That's impossible…"

"So someone's will is in action…," muttered another.

"…It smells like *him*," number 1 rumbled.

"Who?" Number 9 cocked his head.

The man in seat 3 spoke for the first time. "It can't be…"

Number 9 leaned over to his neighbor in seat 10. "Wait, who are we talking about?" he asked, intensely curious.

"Be quiet."

"*Tch.* Whatever. Hey, Axel..." Shut down by number 10, number 9 tried to turn to number 8.

In seat 8, Axel crossed his arms and said nothing.

"What, you too?" Number 9 gave a dramatic sigh.

"Enough, Demyx." That was number 2.

"The time to act is upon us," number 3 said.

A slight frown tugged at Axel's brows.

What if...? What if he'd been able to stop Roxas back then?

If he had told Roxas all the things they kept secret, maybe it wouldn't have come to this. But he'd been unable to betray the organization.

No—he had definitely betrayed them. The one who killed everyone in that castle, who led Riku to Naminé—that was him.

And yet it wasn't a *total* betrayal.

Doubts still swirled inside him. *Why am I here? What do I want? How can I become whole again?*

Even now, he wasn't sure.

What should I have done? What should I do?

Roxas...

"We have to discuss strategy... Axel?"

Startled at being called upon, Axel raised his head.

"You're the one who knows the most about the Keyblade wielders," number 2 said.

Axel nodded.

Back in their nook, the four friends looked at the photos one by one.

"What's going on in this photo?" Hayner wondered.

A grin came to Olette's face. "You just said 'photo'!"

The stolen things and the stolen word had both been recovered.

Roxas eyed the photo in Hayner's hand. "It's me and Wallace. I was his first customer after he took over the shop, so we took a picture together."

"Photos are memories." Olette inspected another one. "You look happy in this one, Roxas."

This picture showed Roxas with Jessie from the Accessory Shop.

"With a girl!" Hayner leaned in to see the photo and whistled.

"So, anybody else notice that all the stolen pictures are of Roxas?" Pence remarked a bit nervously, examining the other pictures.

"Huh? Really?" Olette peered at the photos fanned out in Pence's hand. It was true—Roxas was in all of them. "So that's why everyone thought it was us."

"You mean Seifer didn't go around accusing us after all…?" Hayner said. "What about the real thief? Who was it?"

Roxas shook his head. "I don't know. The pictures were just lying there."

He couldn't really say what that weird creature was. All he knew was…a lot of strange things were happening to him.

"Then how do we prove we didn't take 'em?!" Hayner said, stumped.

"Well, all the pictures were of him… What if the thief actually wanted to steal the real Roxas?" Pence teased.

"Get real. Why would anyone wanna steal a bonehead like him?"

"Excuse you!" Roxas jokingly raised a fist.

"Ack! No!" Hayner covered his head.

"Oh, hey—guys! Here's a picture of all of us." Olette held up a photo of the four of them in front of the haunted mansion.

"Yeah, I look pretty good, huh?" Hayner said.

"Not seeing it." Pence laughed.

Beside them, Roxas stared at the picture.

Right… That picture of all of us together…is important.

Except he couldn't remember when they'd taken it.

From across town, they heard the bells ringing.

"Time to get going, huh?" Olette said. The boys nodded.

"I'll go give everyone's photos back on the way. See you tomorrow!" Hayner left, clutching all the pictures.

"Okay!"

"Later."

Olette and Pence followed him out.

Roxas was the last to leave. Twilight Town's setting sun shone in his eyes.

So bright... Roxas closed his eyes.

And instantly, the world was dark.

"Where am I...?"

He heard a voice inside his head.

"Who's there?" Roxas asked.

"Who are you?"

It was a voice he'd heard before. It was—

—Restoration at 12%—

DiZ felt a presence behind him, but he didn't turn away from the monitor. "Those Organization XIII miscreants... They've found us."

The man in the black coat peered over DiZ's shoulder at the boy's face on the screen. "Why would the Nobodies steal photographs?"

"Both are nothing more than data to them. The fools could never tell the difference. We are running out of time. Tell Naminé she must hurry."

He nodded once in reply and left to speak to Naminé, leaving the sterile, inorganic room and ascending the stairs back to the old mansion. Hardly anyone ever came in here, and the air was musty.

But at the end of the hall on the second floor was her room.

When *he* opened the door, Naminé felt his presence, too, and she closed her sketchbook to hide the drawing she was working on. The room did not match the rest of the house—it was all white, like that castle.

"What were you drawing?" *he* asked, and went to the window.

"...The castle."

"Oh. Well...time's running out."

Naminé looked up and stared at him, but *he* did not look back.

"I promised...," she murmured.

"Huh?"

"Nothing..."

You, the one who chose not to sleep. And Sora, sleeping.

I promised you both, but...

Maybe I wasn't able to keep those promises to you.

Naminé held her sketchbook to her chest and stood up.

THE 2nd DAY

LIGHT, A KEYHOLE, AND A GIANT KEY...

Sora, the boy in the dreams, held that key.

It belonged to Sora... And...that's right, it was called the...

"Key...blade?"

Roxas awoke from the dream and sat straight up, staring at his hands. He remembered the sensation of holding that enormous key. Yesterday, he fought the strange creature with it—the Keyblade.

Was there some connection between the dreams and real life? The key and Sora's weapon in his dreams were the same.

I don't get it...

Scratching his head, Roxas stepped out of bed and got dressed, then ran outside.

To the usual spot, of course.

What he'd seen yesterday...it was like all the dreams he'd been having lately. The stolen pictures, that strange creature, and then the Keyblade.

Roxas picked up a stick on the sidewalk and swung it like a sword.

"What was that about?" he mumbled. Of course, the stick wasn't going to suddenly change into the Keyblade. But then why had his toy sword transformed yesterday?

He sighed and tossed the stick away. It spun through the air and hit a wall—or it should have. But instead it struck a man in a black cloak.

"Oops!"

A deep hood kept the man's face in shadow, and Roxas couldn't tell how angry he was.

"Sorry about that," Roxas said, waving apologetically, but the man turned and walked away without a word.

Roxas had never seen anyone like that around town. But...did he know him from somewhere?

He shook his head at the strange idea. Why would he look at someone he'd never seen before and think they'd met?

"Huh. Weird..." Roxas shrugged and hurried on his way to meet his friends.

Everyone else was sitting where they always did in their hangout, eating sea-salt ice cream bars.

"Morning," Roxas said, the late arrival. Hayner handed him one wordlessly. "Thanks."

He sat on a wooden crate to enjoy it. The ice cream bar, with its unusual salty-sweet flavor, was a specialty of Twilight Town, and not one of the four could resist it.

"Do you guys think we'll always be together like this?" Pence said out of nowhere.

"I sure hope so," Olette replied, as if she'd been wondering the same.

"Huh?" Hayner was mystified. "Where'd that come from?"

"Oh, um, you know... Just thinking out loud." Pence bit into his ice cream bar.

"Well, we probably can't be together forever," Hayner said. "But isn't that just part of growing up? What's important isn't how much we see one another. It's how often we think about one another. Right?"

Roxas looked up at that. Pence and Olette were also staring at Hayner. Silence settled over them for a few moments.

Then Pence laughed. "You get that off a fortune cookie?"

Olette laughed, too.

"Hey! That's it, no more ice cream!" Hayner sprang up, scowling, and glared at everyone else in turn. When he saw that Roxas wasn't laughing at all, his scowl deepened. "Man, what's with all the doom and gloom, you guys?"

"Maybe it's because of that thief yesterday..." Olette looked glumly at the floor.

"Nah—you know what it is? It's 'cos we don't want summer vacation to be over! That's all!" Hayner gestured angrily.

True, they only had a week of summer vacation left.

"So, how about this! We all go to the beach!"

"The beach?" Roxas repeated.

The beach—it made him think of the dreams.

"We haven't been to the beach once all summer!" Hayner went on. "Blue seas! Blue skies! Let's just get on the train and go!"

As usual, Hayner stood like he was delivering a speech. Convinced, Roxas and the others stood up but then hung their heads as something occurred to them.

"No? Aw, c'mon!" Noticing their expressions, Hayner looked upset, too.

"Well...we're all almost broke, so...," Olette explained in a tiny voice.

Summer vacation was almost over, and they'd mostly used up whatever pocket money they had. That was true for all of them, including Hayner.

"Leave that to me!" he declared, undaunted. "Time to hit Market Street!"

With that, Hayner left their hangout at a run.

"So he says, but..." Pence worried, looking back at Roxas.

"Let's just follow him," Roxas said.

Pence and Olette nodded and then dashed outside to catch up.

The three raced through the back streets as if playing tag, and then they saw Hayner paused on the slope leading up to Market Street.

He was looking at the poster advertising the Struggle. "Just two days to go."

The Struggle was a sort of tournament in Twilight Town, in which the contestants battled with a special weapon made for the event. The preliminary rounds were already over. Hayner and Roxas had made it to the semifinals. So had Seifer.

"You and I have to make the finals!" Hayner told Roxas. "And then, no matter who wins, the four of us can split the prize."

"Good call," Roxas said. They shook on it.

"Promise!"

"It's a promise."

Hayner grinned and hopped back from the handshake to face the others.

"Okay! Let's get down to business. One ticket to the beach is nine hundred munny." He took on a math teacher's voice. "So how much for four of us?"

"Three thousand six hundred munny," Olette replied immediately.

"And three hundred each to spend there. What's that add up to?"

This time, Pence answered. "One thousand two hundred munny. So with the train fare, that makes…four thousand and eight hundred munny."

"To spend on what?" Roxas wondered.

"Fried noodles, obviously," Hayner crowed. "What else do you get at the beach?"

"There's always watermelon."

Hayner's mouth twisted in a pout at Roxas's objection. "Too pricey. Watermelons're, like, two thousand munny apiece."

"…Oh."

Now that Roxas had no more objections, Hayner grinned. "So, we need four thousand and eight hundred munny altogether. How much do we have now?"

"I've got eight hundred," Pence said.

"Six hundred and fifty," Olette added, sounding apologetic.

"Only one hundred and fifty," Roxas said. "Sorry."

"That's one thousand and six hundred munny! We just need another three thousand two hundred!" Hayner announced. "Let's find ourselves some odd jobs and earn some dough. We have till the train leaves to earn eight hundred munny each!"

After giving them the assignment, he took off toward the tram common.

"Um…" Olette cocked her head.

"Didn't he say, 'Leave it to *me*'?" Pence shrugged, smiling helplessly.

"Well, whatever. Let's get to work so we can go!" Roxas told them.

They headed for the plaza, where there was a bulletin board that was usually full of Help Wanted ads.

DiZ typed at the keyboard in front of the big computer screen in the dark room.

He approached and spoke behind DiZ's shoulder. "You called me?"

"Your reckless actions will get us in trouble," DiZ said without turning around. "You went there, didn't you?"

"...Yes."

So DiZ already knew that *he* had gone off on his own to see the boy. Roxas—the boy necessary to Sora's awakening.

At this point, to *him*, Roxas was nothing more and nothing less.

"He must seem like a different person, no? And all it took was a bit of meddling with his memories—"

"Did you have an assignment for me?" *he* said, cutting off DiZ.

"Yes... We've encountered a bit of a problem." Finally DiZ turned to face *him*. "I need you to go there again. And make certain your paths do cross..."

Roxas did a few odd jobs, and before too long, he'd earned a solid thousand munny. He headed up to the station.

"Hey, Roxas!" Hayner, Pence, and Olette had finished up their odd jobs, too—they were already there in front of the station.

"What'd you come up with, Roxas?" asked Olette.

"Just this." He handed her the cash he'd made and raised his eyebrows, rather pleased with himself.

"Wow! Nice work, everyone! So, added to what we started with, now we have..." She pulled out a pretty embroidered orange pouch. "Ta-daa! Five thousand munny!"

She let Roxas hold the purse. It was heavy, stuffed with change.

"All right, time to get tickets!" Pence ran ahead with Olette into the station.

Usually Hayner would be the one taking the lead—but he was standing still.

"...We can't be together forever," Hayner murmured. "So we've gotta make the time we do have something to remember."

Roxas was surprised. "Huh?"

"Gotcha!"

As if he was embarrassed by what he'd said, Hayner gave Roxas a friendly punch in the gut and ran after Olette and Pence.

"...Hayner!" Flustered, Roxas started to chase his friend, but his legs gave way beneath him. "Huh?"

This again.

Fighting back that same weird feeling he'd had yesterday, Roxas tensed his legs to keep from falling—when someone grabbed his arm and pulled him.

He yelped in surprise and looked up. It was the same man in the black cloak he'd seen this morning, helping him to his feet.

"Ah...sorry. Thank you...," Roxas said, somehow managing not to fall over again.

The man leaned over and whispered close to his ear, "Can you feel Sora?"

"...Wha—?" Just as Roxas started to ask, the bells of Twilight Town rang.

"Roxaaas!" Hayner poked his head out from the station doors and called to him.

"Coming!" he replied, and turned to the man again.

But no one was there.

He was just *standing right here...*

"Come on, Roxas!" Hayner shouted, and Roxas ran across the plaza.

What was that guy saying? What about Sora?

"Hurry up!"

Roxas charged into the station to find Hayner leaning over the ticket window. Olette was already waiting on the platform.

"Four students!" Hayner blurted at the vendor.

"Roxas, the cash!" Pence said, hopping from foot to foot behind Hayner.

"Got it!" Roxas ran to join them and reached into his pocket. But the purse Olette had entrusted to him wasn't there. "Wha—? It's gone!"

"Huh?!" Hayner turned away from the ticket window.

"He took it!" Roxas headed back out of the station.

"Where are you going?" Noticing that something was wrong, Olette came back down the stairs from the platform.

"You saw me fall just now, right? That's when it got stolen," Roxas said in a rush. "I bet that guy took it!"

Confused, Hayner tilted his head. "What guy?"

"He can't have gotten too far..." Roxas was about to take off and look for the man outside the station, but Hayner grabbed his shoulder.

"What're you talking about? There wasn't any guy," he told Roxas squarely.

"Huh? But..." Roxas trailed off as the station bell rang, announcing a departure.

"The train's leaving," Olette said mournfully.

"Oh... But really—there was someone! He took—"

"It doesn't matter, Roxas..." Hayner let out a deep sigh.

Why did I say that to him...?

He hid his face even deeper under his hood as he headed back to the mansion, his mind wandering.

"Can you feel Sora?"

There was no need to give Roxas that much information. In fact, telling him was a bad idea. And yet, in that moment, when *he* touched Roxas, he couldn't stop himself from asking the question. *He* wanted to know whether Roxas really could feel Sora.

Now that *he* had calmed down a little, the sentiment seemed strange to him.

When would Sora wake up? *He* was getting frustrated with himself, unable to do anything but watch Sora sleep in that capsule.

And *he* felt like he ought to have more memories of the time he'd spent with Sora. Maybe that was why he wanted to know—*could* Roxas feel Sora?

The purse full of munny was in his cloak pocket. They couldn't let the kids go to the beach. They shouldn't even leave the town. That was why *he* had stolen their munny. They had reasons for intervening. Although situations that required their direct intervention weren't supposed to happen in the first place.

Would Sora really wake up?

All year long, *he* had been feeling as powerless as he had back then—back when he could only watch Kairi's helpless sleeping body. *He* had never wanted to feel that way again, so he had ended up fighting a reckless battle...and chosen to become this. To become this form.

Am I doing the right thing...? He didn't know.

But for now, *he* had to believe that he was.

He went through the mansion's gate and opened the front door.

"Welcome back."

It was Naminé, waiting just inside for him.

"What are you doing here?" *he* asked, pushing back his hood.

Naminé smiled sadly. "Because...I found out that you went to see Roxas."

"...Yeah."

That was all *he* said before heading quickly up the stairs.

"It's all right," she told him softly as *he* walked away. "I can feel Sora."

He didn't reply.

* * *

The setting sun was dazzling.

From atop the clock tower above the station, Roxas and his friends could see the entire town. They watched the sunset, each holding a sea-salt ice cream bar.

"It's melting." Olette looked anxiously at Roxas and his ice cream bar, which was starting to drip.

"Oh—sorry…"

Roxas couldn't understand how he'd managed to just lose all that munny.

He was so sure he'd seen that man—but no one else had.

"Hey, forget it already!" Hayner snapped.

"It doesn't make any sense, though." Pence sighed.

Exactly—it makes no sense.

"It is strange," Olette murmured.

"You said it," Hayner agreed.

Even though Roxas told them that a man they couldn't see had stolen their munny, not one of his friends suspected him of lying. But that only made him feel worse. They should have been at the beach eating noodles right now.

"'Can you feel Sora…?'" he mumbled aloud without meaning to.

"Huh?" Hayner squinted at him in confusion, then stood up, having finished his ice cream bar. "Well, we can just try again tomorrow."

"Yeah. Summer vacation still isn't over!" Pence said, trying to encourage him.

"For today, we should probably go home, though." Olette got up, too.

"Yeah…," Roxas said, but he couldn't get himself to smile.

"See you!"

Hayner and Pence began the climb back down.

Olette turned back as she left to follow them. "Don't worry about it, okay?"

Roxas nodded and got to his feet.

The sun was sinking beneath the horizon. It should have been just another usual sunset, but something seemed different to him.

Why? Is something about to change...?

"C'mon, Roxas!" Pence called from below.

"Yeah, coming!" Roxas turned away from the sunset and jumped down the stairs. The last rays of the sun were warm on his back.

—Restoration at 28%—

"Naminé... Hurry," DiZ muttered, staring at the monitor. The number on the screen had risen only slightly, without much in the way of visible change.

Still, compared to the past year, it was fair to call this a significant development.

DiZ became aware that the door was open behind him and swiveled his chair around. "So you've returned."

"Is it really that hard to make a beach?" *he* asked, clutching the orange purse.

"We'd only give the enemy another entry point."

He shrugged and fidgeted with the pouch, tossing and catching it in his palm. "...What should we do with this?"

"We could always get some sea-salt ice cream." DiZ laughed under his breath and turned to the computer again. "You should not bring objects from that town into the real world. Delete it."

He appeared to ignore DiZ, continuing to play with the purse.

CHAPTER 3

THE 3rd DAY

IN DEEP BLACK DARKNESS STOOD A GIRL WITH PALE skin and flaxen hair.

"Who are you?" Roxas asked. But she only smiled, telling him nothing.

And Roxas's consciousness slowly returned from the dark back into the light. His awakening on the third day was gentle and serene.

"Who was that girl…?" he murmured, sitting up in no particular hurry. Suddenly, he had the sense that someone was standing in the corner, and he turned—

"Huh?!"

She was there, the girl from his dream. That couldn't be real. Roxas rubbed at his eyes, and when he opened them again, she was gone.

"A dream…?"

He felt like he'd had another long dream last night. And then, at the end…that girl had appeared.

She had seemed familiar, somehow, and kind.

There was a note left for him in the space below the tracks.

> Meet at the station.
> Today's the day we hit the beach!
> And don't sweat about the munny!

It was from Hayner. Roxas tucked the note in his pocket and left to head for the station. As he was walking down to Market Street, he saw Olette and Pence.

"Hey!" he called. They started to run over to him—but then his vision went funny again. "Huh?"

Olette and Pence had simply stopped midstep, paused like a video.

"Hello, Roxas."

It was the girl from his dream this morning, appearing in front of him while he stood there, stunned.

He could see her more clearly now. Her light-blond hair—the color not too different from his own—fell a little past her shoulders, and she had blue eyes and a white dress. Her skin was so pale it seemed almost translucent.

"Who...?" he began.

She held her finger to her lips and tilted her head. "I wanted to meet you, if I could."

"Me?"

"Yes, you."

Her gaze on him was so intense it almost prickled. Roxas looked away.

And when he did, the world warped.

"Huh...?"

Pence ran up to him. "Olette dragged me along to go shopping."

"You want to come, too?" Olette smiled.

"Um... Just now, there was a..." Roxas glanced at where the girl had been standing. No one was there.

"Roxas, are you okay?" Pence said, worried.

"No—er, yeah... It's nothing..."

Olette gave him a puzzled look. "Well, all right. See you later..."

She and Pence went on toward Market Street.

"That girl...," Roxas murmured.

She said she wanted to meet me. I want to see her again, too, he thought. He had the feeling that she could explain all these bizarre things that were happening to him.

The strange dreams...the weird creature...and that girl.

Roxas took off at a run.

Naminé watched Roxas from atop a building.

We came into being together, like twins. Our hearts are connected to the same place.

No... All the hearts in all the worlds are seeking one single heart—Kingdom Hearts.

But, Roxas, the most important part is...we were born from the same place, in the same way, and the same people are trying to use us.

The organization and DiZ—they both want to use us. Because the way we were created is so special.

And we are seeking the same thing.

Although maybe you've forgotten by now...

"Hey, Naminé."

She looked up at the sudden intrusion. "You..."

Standing there was someone she thought had died in Castle Oblivion—a young man with a black cloak and red hair. "Looks like you and me just keep running into each other."

"...Axel." Naminé met his gaze without backing down.

She was sure Sora had put an end to him back in Castle Oblivion...

"I'm not a ghost, if that's what you're thinking," Axel said with a cocky grin and, along with her, looked at Roxas down below.

"What are you doing here?" she asked.

"Just following orders." His expression went flat as he said this.

"...I see." Naminé frowned and looked away.

"What about you?"

"Me?" She bit her lip.

Me... What do I want to do?

What should I do?

I don't know.

"You're the only one who can save him."

"...What?" She raised her head.

"Got it memorized?"

"Axel..."

He said nothing more, only gave her a faint smile and vanished.

Looking for the girl, Roxas ran to the sandlot.

Seifer and his retinue were loitering there as usual, chatting about something or other. Seifer saw him first. "Hey...Roxas."

But before Roxas could reply, something was swarming him—black shadows on the dirt around him.

"Who dares?" shouted Fuu. The shadows rose up from the ground, taking shape as strange silvery creatures.

"More of them?!" Roxas got ready for a fight.

There were three of them surrounding him, the same kind of creatures as the picture thief.

Seifer was ready, too. "Dunno who they are, but they already crossed the line! Here!"

He tossed Roxas a toy weapon stocked for the Struggle participants.

"Got it!" Roxas caught it and swung at one of the silver things—but just like before, his attacks couldn't seem to hit it. "How—? What do I do...?"

He gripped the toy sword tighter.

"Roxas! Use the Keyblade!" a girl's voice rang out.

It was her.

And then time stopped around him again.

"Huh?!" He looked around, trying to find the source of the voice, and found her on top of a building.

The creatures attacked.

"Roxas!" Naminé called, and this time when he was about to fight back...everything shifted into darkness.

"Wha—? Whoa!"

Darkness swallowed him up, and he fell.

But from above, he could faintly see a light. He flailed his way toward it.

A small white hand reached out for him. The moment he took hold of it, wispy light glowed all around.

"...Who...?" Roxas began.

The girl was floating with him, holding his hand in empty space.

"My name is Naminé." She smiled softly. "Roxas... Do you remember your true name?"

He shook his head. *True name... What does she mean?*

"That's enough, Naminé." A man in a black cloak suddenly appeared from behind her and grasped her arm.

The man's voice sounded familiar to Roxas.

"But if no one tells him, Roxas will..." Naminé looked up at the man's hooded face and trailed off.

If no one tells me...I'll what?

"It's best that he doesn't know the truth."

That voice, it was the same as...

"Can you feel Sora?"

...the voice that had asked him that question.

"Hey! Give our money back!" Roxas shouted.

The man turned away, unhurried. Roxas couldn't quite see his face, but...it seemed like he was laughing a bit.

"Wh-what gives?"

The man let go of Naminé and silently waved his hand. In the dim space behind Roxas, a hole of even deeper darkness opened up.

"Huh?"

The man shoved Roxas hard in the chest, and he fell back into the hole. He yelped...

And then...he came to in the dirt, and the sandlot looked the same as usual.

"Seifer, you should strike a pose, y'know!" Rai was cheering.

"How's this?"

"Awesome!"

After Rai and Seifer's voices came a flash and the click of a camera shutter.

Apparently they were taking pictures with Roxas passed out on the ground.

"One more, y'know!"

Roxas sprang up and rushed at Rai. "Hey, what're you doing?!"

"Keepsake," Fuu said.

"Those freaks in the white jumpsuits are gone, y'know!" Rai told him.

...Gone?

"What...were those things?" Roxas asked Seifer, who was staring at him.

"That's what I wanna know." Seifer nodded decisively. "And if they don't wise up to the rules around here, I might have to take disciplinary action."

"Yeah, Seifer's always looking out for the town!" Rai crowed, as Fuu turned back toward the entrance to the sandlot.

Hayner, Pence, and Olette were there, watching the proceedings.

"Hmph..." Hayner frowned and turned away. Pence and Olette exchanged glances and followed suit.

"Wait up!" Roxas hurried to catch them.

"Hey, no chickening out of the tournament tomorrow!" Seifer called after him.

Roxas pretended not to hear.

When Roxas got back to their hideout, the mood dropped.

"...You hung out with Seifer's gang today?" Pence said, looking a little upset.

"No, it's not like that..." A moment later, Roxas redirected the conversation with a nervous question. "Oh yeah, how was the beach? You guys went today, right?"

"Well...," Olette replied with a glance at Hayner. "It wouldn't be the same without all four of us."

"Sorry..." Roxas hung his head apologetically. Hayner wouldn't even spare him a glance, so Roxas jumped up and approached the other boy. "Hey, what if we go tomorrow? We could get noodles, and—"

Hayner bluntly turned his head away. "I promised I'd be somewhere."

"Ohh… Oh!" Then Roxas finally remembered— Tomorrow was the Struggle tournament.

"I'm outta here." Hayner got up and walked away.

Heavy silence settled in after him, and Olette gave a tiny sigh.

"Roxas…," Pence started.

"Sorry." Roxas hung his head again.

—Restoration at 48%—

He was there with DiZ in the shadowy room. The computer made faint whirring and clicking sounds.

"Was that Naminé made of data?" *he* asked.

"No," DiZ replied, staring at the screen. "Naminé hijacked the data herself. Look what she's done now—completely beyond my control!"

His clenched fist slammed down on the keyboard in frustration. The computer beeped softly.

"Calm down," *he* told DiZ, deflating slightly. *That's the first time I've seen him show any emotion.*

"It doesn't matter," DiZ said. "As long as Naminé fulfills her purpose, we needn't worry about what befalls Roxas."

At that, *he* spun on his heels and began walking away.

"Where are you going?"

He left the room without answering.

Naminé gazed at the sleeping Sora inside the pod.

We have to do this for you to wake up…and for the worlds to wake up, she thought. *Even if we have to sacrifice someone else…Sora must wake up.*

Is that really okay? Is it…right?

We aren't supposed to exist. We never should have been born.

I know that…but I still have a wish.

I want to exist here. And I want to remain in someone's memories.

Hey, Sora… What would you do?

Would you tell us the same things you told the fake one, the puppet—the Replica?

That we're ourselves and no one else? That we have our own hearts inside of us?

And yet…we have no hearts. We seek out hearts because we don't have our own. Is it so wrong to seek out something we've lost?

We have no hearts… But what is a heart, anyway?

I can feel… I feel you. I can think… I think of you.

We can want things… We want hearts.

But doesn't that mean we already have hearts? Or is a heart…something else?

DiZ says that we are "anomalies."

Then what about Axel? Or Ansem?

What about the others from the organization who died in Castle Oblivion?

What is a heart?

I don't know. Sora… Do you know?

The mystery of the one great heart…Kingdom Hearts. It doesn't make sense to me.

Hey, Sora… Can you tell me?

CHAPTER 4

THE 4th DAY

"PROMISE?"

"I promise."

The exchange came to him in a dream…but who was promising who?

Lazing in his bed, Roxas tried to think through the fog of his dreams.

"A promise…," he mumbled, and slowly sat up.

From his window, he could see the usual scene—the town was the same as ever. But today was special. The Struggle was a festival day for Twilight Town.

Then Roxas remembered how upset Hayner had been yesterday. His excitement fell flat. "Aw, what a mess…"

It wasn't that he'd forgotten their promise. He just hadn't remembered right then.

Four competitors had made it to the semifinals—Roxas, Hayner, Vivi, and Seifer.

Those four would fight, and the one who remained would battle the current champion, Setzer.

"Oh, well…I guess I better go." Roxas hopped down from the bed, threw on his clothes, and ran outside.

People from all over town were gathered in the sandlot around the square arena set up in the center.

"Who're you gonna root for?" Pence asked Olette.

"Both of them, silly," she replied.

In the middle of the arena, Wallace—who as the former Weapon Shop manager usually took the role of MC—was discussing something with the tournament's producer.

"Roxas better get here soon," Pence remarked anxiously. Hayner, beside him, hadn't said a word all day.

"You know, Hayner…," Olette started.

"I'm gonna check the rules," he interjected and went to look at the bulletin board where the Struggle rules were posted.

Left behind, Olette and Pence exchanged glances. Just then, there came the loud boom of fireworks, signaling the opening of festivities, and then a fanfare.

The Struggle finals were about to begin.

"There you are, Roxas!" Pence called, spotting him as he ran into the sandlot.

"Sorry! Um…"

"If you're looking for Hayner, he's over there," Olette gently pointed out. Roxas nodded and dashed over to the bulletin board.

"Ladies and gentlemen, Struggle friends of Twilight Town! It's time for the summer's most sizzling clash! That's right—today's the day of the Struggle and title match!" Wallace announced, and the crowd erupted with cheers. Beside the MC stood last year's winner, looking entirely too confident. "Who will be the one to break through the ranks and take on our champion, Setzer?!"

"It's gonna be Seifer, y'know!" Rai shouted.

"And who will win the title match to become our new Struggle champion?"

In contrast to the crowd's fervor, a chill practically emanated from Hayner, who stood balefully in front of the bulletin board.

"Um, Hayner…" Roxas tried to gather the words to apologize for yesterday. But Hayner only shot a brief glance at him and resumed glaring at the board.

"All right! Now it's time to introduce today's fighters! The four bad boys who fought their way through the preliminaries!"

Roxas heaved a quiet sigh under the MC's booming voice.

"Regular finalist and head of the Twilight Town disciplinary committee—Seifer!"

Hearing his name, Seifer raised his chin and took in the arena with a barely visible smirk.

"Completely out of nowhere—who knew he'd make it so far this year? Vivi!"

Vivi headed to the stage from a little ways away from the rest of Seifer's retinue.

"An underground favorite with an attitude—Hayner! It's his first time in the finals!"

"*Hay-ner! Hay-ner! Hay-ner!*" Pence and Olette chanted.

Determined to say something, Roxas tried again. "Hayner, um… About yesterday, I—"

"Get ready. You're up next," Hayner said, and marched briskly toward the arena.

"And fighter number four is a newcomer to the arena, who also happens to be my favorite customer—Roxas!"

Cheers rose all at once from the crowd, and Roxas walked over to the stage, conflicted.

"So, who will win this summer's sweltering Struggle? Who will take home the grand prize, the symbol of our tournament, the Four-Crystal Trophy?"

The four fighters in the arena clustered around the bronze trophy set with four different-colored crystals.

"And not only that, the winner will have a chance to take on our defending champion!"

Setzer nodded in response to the title of "champion."

"Now, let the games begin!" the MC declared. Seifer and Vivi left the arena, followed by Setzer. Only Roxas and Hayner were left. The producer handed them each an official Struggle sword.

Hayner took his and pointed it straight at Roxas.

"Hey… Sorry about yesterday," Roxas told him, with his weapon still dangling from his hand. He felt so guilty, he couldn't stand to meet Hayner's eyes.

After all, he was the one who'd made a promise and forgotten about it.

Seeing Roxas hanging his head like that, Hayner lowered his sword and sighed. "What, you're still worried about that? That was a whole day ago—let it go already."

That sounded like the Hayner he knew.

"Yeah. I have a lot on my mind...," Roxas mumbled.

Too many strange things had been happening to him lately. Those dreams, those weird creatures...and forgetting about a promise he'd made.

"Sorry, dude— Hey, what am I apologizing for?!" Hayner caught himself. That made Roxas smile.

Watching from beside the arena, Pence and Olette happily nodded to each other.

"Ready, Strugglers?" said the producer.

"We're good! Right, Roxas?"

"Yeah."

Hayner and Roxas nodded.

"Our first match of today's Struggle tournament finals will be between two best friends—Roxas and Hayner!"

Roxas ran to the starting position marked by lines in the middle of the arena.

I'm glad he's not mad at me, Roxas thought. *Now I can fight for real.*

The Struggle rules were simple—fight with the provided weapons and whoever gets knocked over first loses. Anyone who didn't fight fair would be disqualified.

"Here goes, Roxas!" Hayner shouted.

"Are we ready?" the MC called. "Let's..."

"Struggle!" the crowd finished, and with that, the battle began.

Hayner didn't waste a second in springing at Roxas.

"Whoa!" Roxas blocked him.

"I've been training in secret!" Hayner grinned. "You're not gonna win against me!"

"Yeah, well, I'm not gonna lose, either!" Roxas counterattacked, and the toy weapon caught Hayner under his chin.

A hint of a frown came to Hayner's face, and Roxas followed up with a fierce body blow.

"Ow-owwww!" Hayner tried to readjust his footing but failed and fell flat on his back.

"And the winner is Roxas!" Wallace ran up to them and took Roxas's hand, pulling it up into the air. Cheers rose from the crowd. "Not even friendship will slow this kid down! And Hayner put up a good fight, too!"

Roxas shook his wrist free and went to Hayner, who was still on the ground. "Are you okay?"

"I lost! Ugh, I can't believe it!" Hayner fumed.

Roxas let out a tiny sigh of relief and pulled Hayner to his feet.

Hayner brushed the sand from his pants. "Man, you really are good."

"It was fun fighting you," Roxas said.

"Not for me, it wasn't!" Hayner screwed up his face in a pout.

"You can have some of my fun. I've got fun to spare."

"How about no."

At some point while they were bantering, Seifer appeared beside them. "Outta my way."

Roxas and Hayner stepped out of the arena, making way for Seifer. From the opposite side, Vivi stared straight up at him, Struggle sword in hand. Under the hood of Vivi's hat, his eyes were hard to see—but they were dark.

He looked at the pod where Sora slept.

Sora was right there in front of him, and yet *he* couldn't sense Sora any more than before. What should *he* do to make that happen?

He reached out, but the wall of the pod stopped his hand so that he couldn't touch Sora, either.

"I can feel Sora."

So said Naminé, the witch who could control people's memories.

Now *he* felt uncertain—was she manipulating his memories?

No, that couldn't be. *He* had chosen to keep his memories. He had chosen not to seal away the darkness in his heart.

That was why he stood facing Sora in this form now. *He* had already abandoned his old name. And not only his name, but his appearance, too.

But…*he* couldn't meet Sora like this. *He* didn't want to, and he couldn't.

He stared at his own hand that had reached out to touch the other boy.

Ditditditditdit, the computer beeped in the dark room.

"What, more scum?" DiZ complained. "No, that's…"

He looked closely at the so-called "scum" on the screen. That was a figure he knew. He would rather not let it get close.

DiZ quietly got to his feet and went up the stairs.

Cheers rang out through the sandlot. In the arena, Seifer was laid out on the ground after one blow from Vivi.

"When did Vivi get so tough?" Hayner remarked next to Roxas's ear.

As Seifer got up, dazed, Rai and Fuu ran to his side.

"Uh…well, the winner is Vivi, ending the fight with a lightning-quick move!" Wallace the MC announced.

Amid the thunderous applause, Seifer slowly approached Roxas.

"Seifer…?" Roxas said tentatively, noticing the grim look on his face.

Seifer's eyes flashed and his voice was low. "That's not Vivi."

"Huh?" Roxas had no idea what Seifer was getting at.

"Take him down," Seifer said icily, and with that he left the sandlot, followed by Fuu and Rai.

Vivi wasn't Vivi? What was that supposed to mean…?

Roxas looked at Vivi standing in the arena, and Vivi returned his gaze. A chill slid down his spine. Vivi's eyes seemed to glow from under that enormous hat he wore—just a little bit frightening.

"It looks like Seifer's withdrawn from the match for third place," the producer told Hayner.

"So that leaves me in third? Aw, yeah!" Hayner struck a victorious pose.

"Ready for the final match, Roxas?" the producer said.

"Uh… Yeah."

As Roxas turned to head for the arena, Hayner thumped him on the back.

"Don't forget about our promise again!"

"I know." Roxas waved to him and went back into the arena.

"Okay, guys. Keep it clean." The producer handed the toy swords to Roxas and Vivi. The two fighters took their starting positions and faced each other.

"And now, the match you've been waiting for—Roxas versus Vivi!"

Roxas lifted his sword, and Vivi stared straight at him without moving a muscle.

"Here we go! Let's…"

"Struggle!" the crowd called out, and in the same instant, Roxas hurtled at Vivi.

But Vivi evaded with a high jump—and Roxas thought he would land farther back, but instead Vivi had launched himself *forward.*

"Whoa!" Roxas barely managed to dodge.

"R…Ro…Roxas…," Vivi called with his sword wavering. That voice didn't sound normal—it was almost *mechanical* somehow.

"Vivi?"

"…Roxas!" Vivi raised his weapon.

Roxas moved to block the strike—and then it happened again.

The world warped…and stopped.

"Not again!" Roxas looked around to see that Hayner, Pence, and

Olette were all frozen with their arms in the air as they cheered. Strangely, Vivi's eyes were glowing.

"…Vivi?!"

Light enveloped his body, and then it changed into one of those weird silver creatures. Two more appeared, like they were seeping out of the air, and fluttered to the ground. Now there were three of them, writhing closer and surrounding Roxas.

"Ugh, these things…" He lifted his toy sword, and this time light flashed along it and transformed it into that oversize key—the Keyblade.

"Guess this means I have to fight them…!" Roxas slashed at the things with the Keyblade. It was the same as when he'd fought the one outside the haunted mansion. They weren't easy to hit, wiggling and dancing around as they did, but now Roxas felt that he *could*. As soon as the Keyblade was in his hand, he could feel himself brimming with power.

I won't lose to these things. Not to a few Dusks.

The Keyblade shone brightly as it scattered the Dusks into nothingness.

When the fight was over Roxas stood, panting heavily, surveying the scene, but time was still stopped. Hayner and the others were still stuck as motionless as mannequins.

"Now what…?" Roxas frowned.

Wait… How do I know what those things are called?

But I do know—they're called Dusks. Our servants.

As he stood there, dazed, he heard the sound of someone clapping from behind him. "Who's there?!"

He turned to see a man in a black cloak.

"All right, Roxas! Fight, fight, fight!" The man's tone had a hint of teasing in it. And while the cloak looked the same, Roxas knew it wasn't the same person who had stolen their money outside the train station.

But who was he…?

The man walked steadily closer. "So you really don't remember, huh?" he said, as if he wanted to confirm something, and pushed back his hood to reveal bright-red hair.

Am I supposed to be remembering something? thought Roxas. *But I've never seen him before.*

"It's me. You know, Axel."

"Axel?" Roxas repeated.

"Talk about blank with a capital *B*. Yeah, this is way too much for Dusks," Axel went on to himself, stretching his arms to either side. At each hand appeared circle-shaped bladed weapons—chakrams.

"Wait a sec," Roxas protested. "Tell me what's going on!"

Axel didn't seem hostile, so he wanted to ask, Why were all these things happening to him? What did it mean?

"This town is his creation, isn't it? So we don't have time for a Q and A. You're coming with me, conscious or not. *Then* you can hear the story."

Roxas could make neither head nor tail of this. Somebody's creation? Going with him? Where?

Axel readied the chakrams and Roxas edged backward. And then—the world warped again.

"Uh-oh," Axel muttered, taking in the scene.

But Roxas couldn't hide his frustration anymore. He hurled the Keyblade at the ground. "What's going *on*?!"

The Keyblade struck with a metallic clang and spun away over the dirt.

He was so angry. All these things were happening, and he was the only one out of the loop. Something was starting, and he had no idea what. It was unnerving—and infuriating. He didn't even know how to stop it.

"...Roxas."

Axel said his name again, and he looked up.

In the same instant, the Keyblade flew back into his hand, as if it was drawn there somehow.

"Number thirteen. Roxas, the Keyblade's chosen one," Axel intoned, his eyes on the shining Keyblade, as he took a fighting stance with his chakrams.

"Fine… You asked for it!" Roxas snapped and fell into stance with the Keyblade, too.

"Yeah! That's more like it!" Axel leaped up and struck with the chakrams, then gave Roxas a flying kick that sent him sprawling.

Axel was far, far stronger than the Dusks. But there was something off about him, Roxas thought as he scrambled to his feet. What was it…? What made him seem so strange?

"Time to heat things up!" A gust of flame shot forth from Axel's hand, knocking Roxas back again. "Ha-ha! Nice, Roxas!"

Axel was laughing—why was he having so much fun?

Actually, fighting him *was* kind of fun.

Roxas was so fed up with all these things happening to him, and he couldn't stand this Axel guy spouting all this weird stuff with his smug know-it-all face—and yet, fighting him like this wasn't all that bad.

What's going on? How am I having fun fighting him? He's obviously holding back against me… Why? What does it mean?

Even as his internal monologue questioned everything, he rushed at Axel and swung the Keyblade.

Grinning, Axel caught the strike with his chakrams. "Hah! There's the Roxas I know!"

"Axel… What do you know?!" Roxas demanded, breathing hard.

Axel's face, up close and personal, looked sad for an instant—or was he only seeing things?

But why—? What did Axel know?

"Can't tell you at the moment," Axel said.

"You can, *too*!" Roxas shouted, and swung the Keyblade up.

And once again, the world twisted and shuddered.

In the middle of the arena, there was a flash of light, along with a strange sound—something electronic. The flash left another man standing there.

He wore red cloth bandages over his face and a red cape.

"...Who's that?" Roxas said.

"So it *was* you...!" Axel jumped up and flung his chakrams at the newcomer, but they only bounced off some kind of barrier, a wall of light.

"Roxas, this man speaks nonsense," the man told him in a deep baritone.

"Roxas, don't let him trick you!" yelled Axel.

Roxas turned back to him. *Trick me? Trick me how?*

Which part is nonsense?

Why are these guys coming to talk to me?

He didn't know. He hardly knew anything.

"Roxas!"

"Roxas!"

"Roxas!"

He couldn't even tell anymore which one of them was calling his name. The voices began to feel like they were coming from inside his head.

The air warped. His head ached.

"Hayner...," Roxas mumbled.

He could say his friends' names.

"Pence..."

He could think of his friends.

"Olette..."

He could feel their friendship.

"Hayner! Pence! Olette!" he cried. The names of the people he wanted to see more than anything, so badly his heart was breaking for them.

And then, the strangeness in the air went away. Axel and the man in the red cape were both gone.

Right in front of him, Vivi was slowly falling.

"What? What just happened?!" shouted Wallace, the MC. A wave of cheering rose from the spectators.

"Huh… How did I get here?" Vivi murmured, and then tottered off.

"Roxas!" Hayner and his other two friends ran up to him.

"Ladies and gentlemen, Roxas, the winner of this year's Struggle!" Wallace announced. Olette bounced with jubilation.

Roxas, however, still looked unhappy.

"Roxas…?" Hayner asked, worried.

"Wha…?"

"Are you okay? You know you won, right?"

"Oh. Yeah…"

So he'd won the Struggle. But he didn't feel like smiling at all.

At that moment, cheers rose from the crowd again. *"Set-zer! Set-zer!"*

The current champion, Setzer, was already there in the middle of the arena, basking in the crowd's appreciation.

"Roxas, it's starting!" Olette said.

Finally, he looked up. But he was more concerned with the things he'd just seen than the battle with Setzer.

Axel…the man in the red cape…the dreams…the Dusks…the Keyblade. And Sora. Was it all connected?

"Okay, you two. Play fair," said the producer. "You're at the top of the bracket."

"There's only room for one up here," Setzer replied.

"Well…may the best man win!"

Roxas went to his starting spot and lifted his weapon. Now that he'd fought that guy—Axel—he felt like he could win.

Setzer leaned in as he passed. "Say, Rucksack… How about you throw the match for me?" he whispered.

"Huh?" he blurted.

At the same time, he heard Hayner shout at him, "Roxas! Focus!"

"Let me win, and I'll make it worth your while," Setzer pressed.

"Get real," Roxas retorted, and the fanfare rang out.

"Roxas, our new rising star, versus Setzer, the defending champion!" the MC announced. "The winner of this match will be this year's champion—that's bragging rights clear until next year, folks! All right, let's..."

"Struggle!"

The instant everyone screamed that word, Roxas dashed within close range of the taller boy and struck as hard as he could at Setzer's torso.

"What?!" Setzer fell backward and landed with an undignified plop. "I'm not supposed to—"

His griping was drowned out by the raucous cheers, which sorted out into one word: "Roxas! Roxas! Roxas!"

Everyone was shouting his name.

"Roxaaas!" Hayner came running, followed by Pence and Olette.

"You did it!" Olette was hopping up and down with excitement.

The townspeople clustered around them.

"Congratulations, Roxas!" The producer handed him the championship belt and then the sizable trophy. The crowd clapped and cheered.

"Ow, ow, ow..." Something had flung Axel back so violently, he had hit the back of his head. Rubbing the sore spot, he got to his feet.

He looked up at the dark city lit only by neon signs. The smell of rain hung in the air, and the "moon" in the sky seemed small from here.

That man, the one who'd been playing mind games with Riku in Castle Oblivion—he was called DiZ.

To a certain extent, Axel understood what had happened in that castle, but he didn't know who DiZ was or what he wanted. He'd gotten into Naminé's head, too.

"*It smells like* him..."

* * *

That's what the leader of the organization had said.

Was there some connection between DiZ and *that man*?

And if Axel was right, was there some staggering secret behind Roxas?

That would mean Axel had made a huge mistake back in Castle Oblivion, which resulted in bringing DiZ and Naminé and Riku together…

"No way…," Axel mumbled to himself, walking along the dark city streets.

This city, cloaked in darkness…and Twilight Town, lit sideways by the setting sun. The two places felt alike. After all, both of them had something to do with Roxas.

As for which place suited Roxas better…Axel wasn't sure.

The clock tower that crowned the station stood about fifty feet above the ground, and the sunset they could see from up there was even more beautiful than usual. The four friends sat on a ledge that stuck out just a little over the clock face, relishing the glory of the day's victory. Clutching the Four-Crystal Trophy, Roxas watched the sinking sun.

He flicked one of the crystals with his fingernail, and it rang softly.

First, he took the yellow crystal from its setting and gave it to Olette. "Ooh!" she cried.

Then he gave the red one to Hayner and the green one to Pence.

Finally Roxas pried out the blue crystal and held it up himself to the setting sun. It sparkled brightly, refracting the day's last light.

"As promised!" he told his friends.

"Thanks, Roxas!" said Pence, likewise holding his green crystal up to the light.

"More treasures for us to share." Hayner held his crystal aloft, his gaze fixed on it, as if offering it to the sky.

"I've got a present for all of us, too." Olette took out four sea-salt ice cream bars.

"All right!"

Olette distributed the treats, and just as Roxas accepted his, he slipped.

"Wha—? *Augh!*"

As he fell from the height of the clock tower, everything he could see shrank into darkness.

FRAGMENT
Wherever You Are...

A GIRL IN A SCHOOL UNIFORM WALKED AT AN EASY pace to the beach. The path wound from the sleepy houses in town over a small hill that blocked the ocean from view.

The breeze ruffled the girl's red hair. In the evening, the wind would change, blowing out from the land back over the sea.

"Hey, Kairi!" another girl called.

Kairi paused and turned around. The other girl, who wore the same uniform, was jogging to catch up. Her brown hair, curling upward at the ends, bounced with every step.

When she caught up, Kairi turned back to the sea and they strolled toward it together, slow in the twilight.

"Do you feel like going out to the island? We haven't been in so long," her friend Selphie said. "Tidus and Wakka are all wrapped up in their ball game, and they won't go with me..."

"Sorry," Kairi replied. "But not today."

"Aw, why not?"

They'd almost reached the crest of the hill.

"Do you remember those boys who used to hang out with us?" Kairi said.

Selphie had to think for a moment, cocking her head, before she recalled a name. "...Riku?"

"Yeah." Kairi nodded, looking at her expectantly.

"What happened to him, anyhow? I sure do miss him."

"He's far away. But I know we'll see him again."

We will, Kairi told herself. *He promised.*

"Yeah," Selphie agreed. "Of course we will."

The sun was about to set, but the breeze was still coming in from the sea, messing up their hair.

"What about the other boy?" Kairi prompted without looking at Selphie, her gaze fixed on the ocean.

The other boy. Right—there was another boy, too. I'm sure there was.

"What other boy?" Selphie looked confused.

So she doesn't remember. Kairi kept staring at the water. Out there, little islands sat sprinkled atop the blue sea.

Up until a year ago, they would all climb this hill and sprint full speed down to the beach almost every day. There were little boats at the docks for the kids to row out to the islets, called the Destiny Islands.

"The one who was with Riku and me all the time," Kairi said. "We played together on that island. You know, for a while I could hear his voice...but now it's gone."

Selphie looked up at her, mystified.

"Now I can't remember his face or even his name. I feel awful about it. So I told myself, I'm not going to the island until I remember everything about him."

"Are you sure you didn't make him up...?" Selphie said.

Kairi didn't answer. The sun was just touching the horizon. Its last rays streamed toward her, and the wind went calm.

All she could see was light. She heard the sigh of the waves, like a name...

"Naminé?"

A voice spoke from somewhere...and pulled her into darkness.

A boy stood there in the endless darkness.

"Naminé? What's happening to me?" asked the chestnut-haired boy.

Kairi answered with a question. "Who are you...?"

The boy looked a little troubled at this.

"And that's not my name," she corrected him, looking him in the eyes. "I'm Kairi."

"Kairi... I know you. You're that girl he likes." He looked down.

He? He who?

"Please give me a name!" she practically begged.

"I'm…Roxas."

"Okay, Roxas… But can you tell me *his* name?"

Just then, everything seemed to haze and warp, like the picture on a TV with bad reception. Kairi blinked.

The boy was gone. There was nothing in any direction but darkness. And yet, there was something gentle about this darkness.

"C'mon, tell me!" she cried.

A voice answered her:

"You don't remember my name? Thanks a lot, Kairi!"

"Huh?"

It was a boy's voice—but she couldn't see anyone.

"I guess it can't be helped… Fine, I can give you a hint!"

He kept talking, but static seemed to rise again.

"It starts with an S!*"*

Starts with an S?

Kairi was about to ask for more hints, but a light from somewhere pierced the darkness. It grew until it covered everything, bright enough to hurt her eyes—and then she fainted again.

Naminé—the sound of waves…

"Kairi!"

Selphie was staring at her, worried.

Right… They were on the path to the beach. Kairi let Selphie help her up and gazed at the ocean again.

"Kairi?"

The islands floated on the water, and beyond them, the sinking sun.

"Hey—Kairi?!"

She began sprinting down the hill toward the beach. *This is what we always did, running down the hill.*

Through the dune grass onto the sand. *We always ran barefoot, too.*

"Kairi!" Selphie struggled to keep up, out of breath by the time she made it onto the beach.

Without turning around, Kairi took a small bottle out of her satchel. The bottle contained a piece of paper, folded up tight.

"What's that?" Selphie asked.

With a tiny smile, Kairi set the bottle down into the water. The receding wave carried it away, and it began to drift slowly out to sea.

"A letter. I wrote it yesterday to the boy I can't remember. I said that no matter where he is…I'll find him someday. And then, when I finished writing, I remembered we made a promise—an important one. This letter is where it starts. I just know it."

She smiled, seeing the bottle bob atop the waves.

"Wow…," Selphie said. "I hope he gets it."

"He will."

They both watched the bottle float away.

It'll reach you. I'm sure of it.

"It starts with an *S*…," Kairi murmured, and then raised her voice into the sea breeze. "Right, *Sora*?"

—Restoration at 79%—

"Sora is coming back."

At that, Axel looked up.

The one who had spoken was number 3 in Organization XIII.

"Then—," Axel started, but bit down on the question he wanted to ask. *Then what's going to happen to Roxas?*

It was an abruptly called meeting. He had suspected what it would be about, but there was no need to reveal his own agenda.

"So, we have no choice but to destroy number thirteen," number 7 pronounced coldly.

"Indeed, if he has no intention of returning to us," number 3 said.

The others were silent, briefly.

"So we have to eliminate the traitor, is that it?" That was number 9—Demyx.

Axel's eyebrow twitched. The words grated on his nerves. Actually, everything the others said irritated him.

The fact that the members of Organization XIII shared the same goal did nothing to make them close with one another. Some among them had been friendly back when they were human. Whether that made any difference to the others, Axel didn't know, and he didn't need to know.

For a member of the organization, there was only one goal—to obtain a heart.

But just because we have no hearts doesn't mean we feel nothing, thought Axel. *We just know that we're...incomplete somehow. When we were told that what we each lack is a heart, it made perfect sense. Because we definitely lack* something.

"Axel," number 1 said.

Axel stood in response to the rare occasion of their leader clearly addressing someone.

"You will eliminate Roxas."

Keeping his mouth shut, Axel looked back at number 1.

"Did you not hear me, Axel?"

"No, I heard you perfectly." A smirk curled the corner of his lips, and then he vanished from the hall.

THE 5th DAY

IN THE WHITE ROOM IN THE MANSION, NAMINÉ SAT sketching quietly.

Now...what to draw today?

"Oh...!" A tiny exclamation left her as she looked up from her sketchbook.

She'd heard something just now—a voice.

"...Sora?" it said.

A hint of sorrow crept into her expression, and she focused on her sketchbook again. Then the door opened.

"Naminé."

It was *him* standing in the doorway. *He* seemed a little out of breath—unusual for him. But Naminé already knew why.

"...You felt Sora?"

He had too many questions of his own to answer. "What happened?"

"I don't know."

"...Oh."

Naminé noticed that *he* had something in his hand—a blue crystal. "What's that?"

"It...belongs to him." *He* held the crystal up to the light, making it gleam and sparkle.

"Him...?"

"Roxas." *He* tucked it into his pocket and turned away.

"Did you go to see Roxas again?"

"I didn't see him."

Naminé would have liked to know how *he* had taken something belonging to Roxas without seeing him. She asked a different question instead. "Then did you run into anyone else?"

"Anyone else?" *He* turned to face her again. "Who are you talking about?"

"You'd know if you did. Don't worry about it," Naminé replied, looking at one of the drawings she had pinned up on the wall.

It showed a chestnut-haired boy and a red-haired man, both wearing black cloaks.

"...If you say so." With that *he* walked out.

Why are he *and I always shying away from talking about anything important?* Naminé wondered. *We can never say what we need to say to each other. We still can't.*

DiZ faced the screen in the computer room beneath the mansion. Sensing another presence, he turned. "There you are. His progress is astounding." He gestured at the number on the screen.

"What happened?" *he* asked, and took a blue crystal from his pocket to put it into the embroidered purse he'd taken the other day.

"Naminé's encounter with Roxas put his heart in contact with Kairi's," DiZ explained. "And that, in turn, affected Sora—you see?"

"Naminé...? She's something else," *he* remarked, fidgeting with the purse.

"She wasn't born like other Nobodies," DiZ explained flatly. "She can tamper with the hearts and memories of Sora and those aligned with him."

Naminé was special.

The darkness in one's heart could become a Heartless. When it did, a Nobody was born. But Naminé had originated from a girl with no darkness in her heart—her very existence was unique.

"...But whose Nobody is she?"

DiZ smiled at the question behind his bandages. *That's right—I haven't told* him *yet.*

"I could tell you. But first...perhaps you could tell me your true name?"

He pushed back his hood. The features *he* revealed were gold eyes and silver hair. "It's Ansem."

Whatever answer DiZ had thought he might receive, Ansem

wasn't one of them. Such an answer could only be in jest, or so it sounded to him. "Heh-heh...ah-ha-ha-ha! It's an honor, Ansem!"

As DiZ went on chuckling, *he* drew up his hood again and left the room.

He was falling through endless darkness.

Falling, and falling, and falling.

Forever—

Roxas woke with a start, drenched in cold sweat. He felt a little better seeing himself at home in his own room.

"Just a dream...," he mumbled under a huge sigh.

Or was it?

He'd slipped and fallen from the clock tower—and he couldn't remember anything after that.

"Which parts...were the dream?"

He couldn't tell dreams from reality.

He'd dreamed of that girl again. And he'd seen her in town the other day. Now he wasn't sure what was real.

"Naminé...Keyblade...Axel...Sora...Kairi...Riku...Ansem..." He listed all the names to himself.

He'd met Naminé. He'd battled using the Keyblade. He'd fought Axel.

And then there was the man swathed in red bandages. And the man in the black cloak.

Kairi, the girl Sora liked. Riku, Sora's friend.

Which parts had he dreamed? He didn't know.

Roxas clambered out of bed and listlessly started to get dressed.

Hayner and Pence and Olette. Those three were his friends, and that was unquestionably real.

So of course he had to go to their haunt—there were only three days of summer vacation left. And they hadn't been to the beach yet.

Roxas left his room.

* * *

A passing train rumbled above their hangout. Olette was arguing with Hayner, which didn't happen often.

"We've only got three days of summer left!" shouted Hayner. "Don't even talk about that assignment!"

"But we agreed that we'd get it finished today. Didn't we, Roxas?" She looked to him for support.

Roxas was no help. "Um, yesterday...didn't I fall off the clock tower?"

Olette flinched at the idea.

"You wouldn't be here if you did!" Hayner said.

"Man, it was a close one, though." Pence laughed.

So he hadn't fallen...? Roxas cocked his head. He was so sure he had—or was that just another dream?

"Stop changing the subject!" Olette scolded them.

"All right already..." Hayner stood up with a sigh. "You win. We'll do the homework. Today's the day for a pain-in-the-butt independent study project."

Roxas had completely forgotten that there were any vacation assignments until now. Only three more days, and then it was back to school.

School? Wait, was I ever going to school?

"So, any bright ideas for a topic?" Hayner prompted.

Roxas looked up at that. "Maybe we could study the stuff that's been happening to me. You know, the dreams, and those silver things—"

Hayner cut him off. "Forget it."

"How come?" Roxas protested.

Pence and Olette exchanged glances.

"You know how things have been weird with you and around town since those photos got stolen?" Hayner said.

Roxas nodded.

"Tomorrow, everyone's gonna search the town and find out what's been going on," Pence said brightly.

"Lots of people are helping out," Olette added, giving Roxas a reassuring smile.

This was the first Roxas had heard of it. "All that for me?"

"Well, yeah. Why wouldn't we?" Hayner crossed his arms and puffed out his chest.

A town-wide investigation...for me? That makes me really...happy. Everyone was thinking of him, after all.

Noticing that Roxas looked a bit bashful, Pence spoke up. "So, there's this weird rumor going around—you wanna hear it?"

"A weird rumor?" Olette said.

Pence made a grim face for effect and went on in a creepy hushed voice, like an old woman telling a story at a campfire. "You know the stone steps at Sunset Station? We take them all the time without even thinking about it... But there's something very strange about them... You'll count a different number of steps going up and down!"

"Seriously?" Hayner blurted.

"And there are six more weird stories like that," Pence said in his normal voice. "It's like the Seven Wonders of Twilight Town."

"We can investigate those for our project! Pence, you're a genius!" Hayner gushed.

Olette nodded, too.

"There might be even more urban legends around," Pence added. "Let's split up and look into it."

Hayner dashed to the entrance. "Okay! Olette and I will go find some new rumors. C'mon!"

"Slow down, Hayner!" Olette called, chasing him.

"That leaves you and me, Roxas," Pence said. "Let's try the train first. To the station!"

Roxas nodded, and they left their hangout together at a run.

* * *

Twilight Town had two train lines—the one that ran to the beach and another local line that went through town. The other end of the local line was Sunset Station over in the residential terrace.

"Here I go, Pence!" Roxas hopped on a skateboard he found sitting outside and took off for the station.

"Hey, Roxas! No fair!" Pence tried run after him.

It had been a while, actually, since he'd ridden a skateboard. He liked the wind on his face as he zipped along the streets.

When he thought about tomorrow, he felt better than he had in a while.

Tomorrow, everyone would come out to help him search for the secrets behind all these strange things happening to him. Knowing that, he felt like not even the dreams or those silver creatures could bother him.

He sped through the city on the skateboard and waited in front of the station for his friend to catch up. "Took you long enough, Pence!"

Pence came running, breathing hard, his shirt soaked through with sweat, since he was a bit on the heavy side. He huffed and glared reproachfully at Roxas.

"Oh… Sorry." Roxas did feel bad at that. He hung his head apologetically.

"Aw, it's fine. C'mon, let's get on the train." Pence smiled at him and climbed the steps to the station, then pulled the door open. Roxas followed him in.

He was pretty sure that the local line had no fare. They continued up the steps to the platform to find that a train to Sunset Station was waiting.

"And now…we hunt for the Seven Wonders!" Pence said in his creepy voice, grinning with anticipation.

"Not without us!" Hayner announced, storming the platform with Olette.

"Whoa, you find new rumors already?" asked Pence.

"Nothing on Market Street," Olette said.

"You twerps aren't gonna scoop us. We're going to the terrace, too!" Hayner jumped into the train car.

Olette looked exasperated. "Honestly… It's not a race, Hayner."

"It is now!" Hayner declared, poking his head out.

Roxas and Pence exchanged glances. "I guess we're all going," Roxas said. Pence and Olette stepped onto the train with him.

The familiar rumble of the train was relaxing, though Roxas usually heard it from outside rather than in.

The four of them all sat apart, staring out the windows. The light from the lowering sun shone softly into the train car.

"It's so pretty…," Olette said, and took something out of her pocket—her yellow crystal, the one Roxas had given her from the Struggle trophy. Smiling brightly, she held it up to the light, where it sparkled.

Hayner and Pence followed suit and took out theirs. The crystals all glistened in their respective colors.

Roxas stuck his hand in his pocket—but the crystal wasn't there. He couldn't find it anywhere. His blue crystal… Where could he have put it?

The others had theirs, sparkling in the low sunlight. Roxas looked at them blankly.

Come to think of it, he had lost something else like this when he had every reason to think he had it—Olette's purse.

The photos, Olette's purse, and now his crystal.

Why do my things keep disappearing?

The moment the train came to a halt, Hayner jumped up. "C'mon, Olette! Hurry!"

She paused to exchange glances with Roxas and Pence, then ran after Hayner.

"I say we take our time," Pence said blithely, stepping out to the platform, and Roxas followed him.

Sunset Station was on a rise overlooking the neighborhood. The stone steps that led up the slope were supposed to be one of the Seven Wonders.

"This is it, right? The stone steps that count differently going up and down?" Roxas said, peering down the steps.

"Um, actually..." Pence grinned as he examined the steps. "It's the stupidest thing ever, but..."

"What?" Roxas said.

Pence started walking down them. "The one who counted them was Rai. And he's like, 'Every time I count, it's *different*, y'know!' So there it is." He shrugged.

If Rai was counting, he *would* get a different number every time. "You mean...he just counted wrong?" Roxas sighed.

Pence nodded.

Roxas slumped in disappointment. "Ugh, really..."

"Hey, there's other weird stuff out there," Pence said. "In fact, I thought Olette might bring it up for the school project, so I put 'em all on a map."

"Really? Nice work, Pence!"

Pence unfolded a map and Roxas leaned in to look at it. There were five spots in the neighborhood marked with an X. One was the steps they were standing on.

"What about the last two?" Roxas said.

"I'll tell you after we investigate the first five." Pence smirked.

He walked down the hall that led to the room where Sora slept. Pods lined the hallway, but only two were in use. *He* looked up at the two fast asleep inside them, the king's loyal servants, Donald and Goofy. The others were all empty, though some of them showed traces of past use. But whoever had slept in them had nothing to do with him, *he* thought. Even though *he* sensed a powerful scent very similar to his own.

He opened the door. Unlike the corridor, this room was full of serene white light. In the middle of the space, Sora was sleeping.

Up until now, *he* hadn't been able to feel Sora without looking straight at him. Today was different.

Today, *he* had felt Sora all day. *He* could feel that Sora was returning to his heart.

He wanted to see Sora. *He* wanted to see Sora *awake*, and soon.

But the way *he* was now—he couldn't look Sora in the eye. Maybe *he* could never let Sora see his face again.

He felt like he hadn't truly met Sora again since that night—the night when their island was destroyed.

Could Sora ever truly forgive him?

He pushed back the hood of his cloak to show his silver hair and looked up at Sora with amber eyes.

This form that *he* hated more than anyone…

He had given his name as Ansem to DiZ. It wasn't quite a lie.

That's right… I am Ansem. The one who covered the world in darkness.

His eyes remained fixed on Sora.

Just like the stone steps, the other four wonders on Pence's map turned out to be nothing remarkable.

The so-called "friend from beyond the wall" rumor came from some kids who threw a ball and didn't realize it had only bounced off the wall back to them, and the moans from the tunnel had been Vivi practicing for the Struggle. The report of the wiggling bag arose thanks to a dog who liked to climb into bags and jump around. The mysterious doppelgänger was actually one's own reflection in a sheet of water from a fountain.

"You know...if you actually investigate them, these wonders aren't exactly wonderful," Roxas complained with a sigh.

"I know, I know. But this next one's gonna be really great! Wonder number six!" Pence said cheerfully, just as Hayner and Olette came running.

They announced their findings in rapid succession.

"We got another lead!"

"The Ghost Train Mystery!"

Pence shrugged. "Yeah, everyone knows about wonder number six."

"Well, *I* didn't!" snapped Hayner, crestfallen that their hard-found scoop wasn't much of one.

"Where's the train run?" Roxas asked Pence.

"They say you can see it from Sunset Hill."

Sunset Hill, at the edge of the terrace, was famed as the best viewing spot for Twilight Town's sunsets.

"Well, what's the mystery?" Roxas wondered.

"They say the train is always empty...," Pence said in his creepy voice again. "No driver, no conductor, no passengers—not a soul aboard."

"It comes at nightfall," Olette added.

"Let's go check it out!"

They nodded at Hayner's directive and headed for Sunset Hill.

From up on Sunset Hill, they could see the sun sinking into the distant sea. To see the train tracks they had to go to the edge of a steep precipice, which was cordoned off with a low fence.

"If the rumors are true, it'll be here any minute," Hayner said, plopping himself down on the ground.

Beside him, Roxas lay on his stomach, dozing off. Olette was stretched out on the ground, too, while Pence slowly sat down with his legs extended in front of him.

"We've gotta make it to the beach next year," Olette murmured, watching the sunset.

Hayner leaned forward. "Yeah. Better get jobs the second vacation starts."

Next year… Right. Next year there would be another summer vacation. This one was almost over, but they'd have next year to try again.

Letting his mind wander, Roxas found that the perfectly obvious fact cheered him up.

"Oh, look. A bunch of slackers. What are you even doing out here?"

The four friends turned at the sudden voice to see Seifer.

"What d'you care?" Hayner retorted, sounding enormously annoyed.

"I don't. Tell me anyway."

"We're waiting for the ghost train," Pence said without a care in the world.

"Waiting for the ghost train?" Seifer burst out laughing.

It was mean laughter, and Roxas couldn't stand it. He got to his feet and glared daggers at Seifer.

"Why does looking at you always tick me off?" Seifer remarked, cracking his neck.

"I dunno. Maybe it's destiny."

"Destiny, huh? In that case, let's be friends." Strangely, Seifer's expression softened. "I don't feel like cooperating with destiny."

"When have you ever cooperated with anything?" Hayner said.

Seifer brought his fist to his chest and cracked a smile, then turned away.

"Seifer…?" Olette called after him.

"I know. Tomorrow." Seifer waved without looking back at them and ambled off.

Then, from the distance, Roxas heard a train whistle.

"There it is!" he cried, running up to the edge.

"...Roxas?" Hayner said quietly from behind him.

"The train! It's here!"

There it was, slowly passing before him. Unlike the trains that went around town, this one was violet. He could see through the windows in the very front to where the driver should have been—and no one was there.

"It's true!"

The train plunged into a tunnel and disappeared from sight.

"There's really no one aboard..." Roxas whirled back to the others. "What's the catch? There's gotta be some dumb explanation, right?"

His friends didn't look at him—they exchanged glances with one another. Hayner seemed dubious, Pence a bit surprised, and Olette worried.

And none of them said a word.

"So it's real, right? Let's go to the station!" Roxas broke into a run.

"Slow down, will ya, Roxas?!" Hayner chased after him, with Pence and Olette close behind.

On the hill lit by the sunset glow, a man in a black cloak appeared from a cloud of static and silently trailed Roxas and his friends.

When they ran up the steps to Sunset Station, Roxas was completely winded, barely even remembering to breathe.

The violet train was stopped at the platform.

"Let's check out the inside!" As Roxas lurched for the train doors, Hayner caught his arm. "What's wrong?!"

"Um... You'll get hurt." Hayner was looking past him at the train—or rather, at the empty space above the track.

Roxas looked back again and saw that there was no train. "But—huh?!" *What? It was just there!*

"The train will be arriving shortly." The station announcement echoed over the platform. A local train came in and eased to a stop.

The doors opened, and passengers stepped out, including Fuu and Rai.

"A train came in from the beach, and it didn't have a driver. Right?" Roxas said blankly.

"Let's go," Pence said, more for his own benefit than anyone else's.

"But you saw it, right?"

"C'mon."

Beside them, Hayner shook his head and pushed Roxas toward the local train.

"Didn't you see it?!" Roxas protested.

"...No. We didn't." Hayner's voice was low as he shoved Roxas aboard.

The other train...had never been there. Roxas was the only one who had seen it.

The bell signaling departure rang, and Olette and Pence hopped into the train car, too. The train took them back into the center of town.

None of them spoke during the train ride, nor as they disembarked at Central Station and walked outside.

Finally Hayner spoke up, trying to shake off the gloomy mood. "Well, time to go home and work on that project."

"The rumors were all bogus. The end," Pence said with a worried glance at Roxas.

"We can still make it sound good if we write about all the work we did," Olette pointed out gently.

Roxas stared miserably at the ground and mumbled, "But what about the last one—the seventh wonder?"

"Who cares?!" snapped Hayner.

Roxas ignored him. "C'mon, Pence," he said, approaching the stockier boy.

"Fine. Whatever!" Hayner angrily ran off.

Olette stared after him and then turned. "Roxas...?" she said anxiously.

But Roxas turned his back on her and stared pointedly at Pence.

"It's at the haunted mansion." Pence sighed.

"The haunted mansion?"

Pence and Olette exchanged a look and followed Hayner.

I don't get it... Why is everyone acting like this? Roxas thought. *The train was there. It stopped at the platform. Does this really mean no one else could see it?*

Then why was I the only one who could?

He didn't understand any of it.

As the sun's red glow streamed over the plaza in front of the station, Roxas took off for the haunted mansion.

Naminé had finished her drawing of a redheaded girl in the middle of her sketchbook page.

She set down her pastels with a small sigh and raised her head.

The room was covered with the drawings she'd done in the past year. They were all scenes she had come to know from Sora's memory, even though she had nothing like that of her own.

I have no memories of my own...

There was no breeze, and yet she had sensed the curtains stirring. Naminé stood up.

When she peeked out beyond the edge of the curtains, she saw *three* people outside.

She quietly closed her eyes and thought of him—the one who was like another version of herself.

Do I feel sorry for him...? Then should I feel sorry for myself?

No...there's no reason to pity me. I got to meet Sora, after all.

But, he——

Something distorted the air in the white room. And then... Naminé vanished.

* * *

He ran all the way to the mansion, hardly pausing for breath. Out there it was as hushed as ever.

Nothing was there… Nothing was going to happen. Roxas stared at the gate with its enormous lock.

"You know…," a voice said from behind him.

Roxas jumped. "Ack! …Wh—? Pence?"

It was his friend standing there.

"We were gonna check out the mansion tomorrow. It's the most suspicious place, after all." Pence acted as if nothing at all was amiss, and he was staring up at the house, too.

"Oh. Right…" Roxas hung his head, a little depressed to hear yet another thing he'd missed.

"Even Seifer's gang is gonna help."

Surprised, Roxas looked up. "Seifer?"

"Yeah." Pence laughed a bit awkwardly and shrugged. "Hayner asked him to."

Roxas hadn't imagined that Seifer would help with all that. Actually—he hadn't imagined that Hayner would even ask him to.

Looking at Pence's weak smile, Roxas began to feel bashful, and he turned back to the mansion. He could see white curtains fluttering in a second-story window.

"So, Pence… What're we looking for?"

"Um, well, they say there's a girl who appears in a second-story window, even though nobody lives here."

Roxas stared harder up at the window.

"Roxas…"

He thought he heard a girl's voice from somewhere.

It was that girl—Naminé.

"Roxas?" He heard Pence's voice layered on top of hers. The world warped and twisted.

But it didn't feel unpleasant like usual.

Naminé was calling him...

Naminé gazed down the long table. Roxas was gradually being "drawn" there, like a painting. Although she wasn't sure that was the right word.

But to say he was being painted into the room was closer to the truth than to say he was simply appearing.

"Naminé?"

He called her by name, and she replied with a silent smile. He seemed a tiny bit startled as he scanned the room, and his eyes fell on a particular drawing. "This is...me? And that guy Axel...?"

It was Naminé's drawing of Roxas and Axel, standing side by side.

"You're best friends," she said.

Right. Those two had been friends—well, Axel believed they still were. Roxas was his only friend and his best. And Axel was the same for Roxas—probably.

"Cut it out." Roxas shook his head.

"Don't you want to know the truth about who you really are?"

I would, Naminé thought. *If I were him, I'd want to know. Why was I created? Why am I here? I did want to know once.*

"Well, no one knows that better than me," Roxas retorted.

Naminé looked down. "Of course..."

"But...I don't get what's been happening lately."

At that, she pointed to one of the pictures on the wall—a drawing of Sora with Donald and Goofy. "You know those three, don't you?"

"Oh yeah...Sora, Donald, and Goofy," he murmured, examining the picture. "They're from the dreams."

Naminé took in a big breath and spoke slowly. "About a year ago...some things happened, and I had to take apart the memories chained together in Sora's heart. But now, I'm putting them all back, just the way they were. It's taken me a long time, but pretty soon Sora will be his old self again. The process is affecting you, too."

"You mean...the dreams?"

"Yes. You and Sora are connected."

Directly behind Roxas there was a drawing of him and Sora, holding hands. Naminé's eyes fixed on it as she continued. "In order for Sora to become wholly himself again...he needs you."

Because Sora hasn't been whole since then. Since the moment you were released from his heart.

"Me? What for?" Roxas said.

"You hold half of what he is. He needs you, Roxas."

Downcast, she thought, *But who needs me?*

"Naminé... Who are you?"

She raised her eyes at him again. "...I'm a witch with power over Sora's memories and those of the people around him."

Roxas frowned. "A witch?"

"That's what DiZ called me. But I don't know why I have this power... I just do. I'm not even sure there is a right way for me to use it." She shook her head. *I don't know much of anything for sure.*

But that was why she wanted to know how Roxas felt. What he would do.

"Yeah...I can't help you there." Bewildered, Roxas smiled awkwardly. She couldn't help but smile back.

They shared a few moments of quiet. Then, as if he couldn't bear to look at her for too long, Roxas turned his attention to the room again. Among the significant number of drawings tacked up on the wall, the ones of men in black cloaks got his attention. Naminé noticed something about those men tugged at his mind. But right now he probably didn't know any more about them than she did.

"It's funny... Suddenly I feel like I don't know myself at all," Roxas said. "I guess I would like to know... What do you know that I don't?"

"You..." Naminé raised her eyes and told him, "You aren't supposed to exist, Roxas."

His eyebrows drew tight. "What...? How could you say something like that? Even if it was true!"

Seeing him upset filled her with sorrow, too. What she'd said to him was also true of herself.

You and I...neither of us were supposed to exist. Just like them.

"I'm sorry," Naminé apologized, looking away. "I guess...knowing doesn't make a difference."

If Roxas didn't need to know, there was no reason for her to keep talking to him.

The instant she felt that, Roxas disappeared from the room.

There's nothing more we can talk about. It's better if he doesn't know all this. I never wanted to, either.

"Roxas? Roxas!"

Hearing Pence's voice, Roxas twitched.

"Huh?" He looked around and Naminé was nowhere to be seen. He was out in front of the haunted mansion.

"Didja see her?" Pence demanded.

"The window..." Roxas pointed to the second-story window, where the curtains were fluttering. He felt as if Naminé was still watching him from up there... But he couldn't see her.

"Aw, weak. That's just the curtains moving. I bet it's all drafty 'cos the place is falling apart."

"...Yeah." Roxas nodded.

That had to be a dream just now.

I was never supposed to exist...? Why would she say that?

"Well, let's head back to our spot. Hayner and Olette are waiting." Pence headed into the forest, and Roxas followed.

Naminé...

* * *

"You aren't supposed to exist."

Roxas glanced back at the mansion once more. There was no one at the window.

He walked slowly through the mansion.

The train… That really hadn't been necessary. *He* couldn't understand why DiZ would deliberately do something so uncalled for.

There was a soft patter of footsteps behind him. *He* turned to see Naminé, miserably hanging her head, thin shoulders trembling.

"…Naminé?"

"You once said the darkness would lead you." She didn't look at him as she spoke, and her voice was barely audible.

He realized that she might be crying.

"Your darkness belongs to you… You need it."

"What are you getting at?" *He* took a step closer to her.

"The world…*needs* darkness. Light exists because there is darkness. So what about us?" Finally she looked up at him. "What about us?"

We are neither darkness nor light…, Naminé mused.

Why were we even born?

Olette greeted them back at their hideout below the tracks. "Hey, guys. How'd it go?"

"The true identity of the girl in the window is…a curtain flapping in the wind," was Pence's mock report.

Roxas looked for Hayner, but he didn't seem to be there. *Is he… mad at me again?*

"I figured it was something like that," Olette said. "So the report's already done."

"All right!" Pence jumped for joy.

"So, wanna go find Hayner? He's probably at the station." Olette had noticed the way Roxas was looking around. She went up to him. "You know, we only have two more days together."

"Huh?" Something about the words felt like they carried some special meaning.

"You know, of summer vacation," Olette said.

"Oh… Right."

Only two more days of summer vacation. School would be starting before they knew it…

He paid a visit not to the computer room, but to one of the rooms in the mansion. Since Sora's condition had settled, DiZ didn't spend as much time in front of the screen. Apparently he was nearly finished with those documents he'd been typing up, too.

"Why did you let him see the train?" *he* asked.

At the question, DiZ raised his head with a hint of a smile. "Because he missed the trip to the beach."

"Hmph… That's almost kind of you."

DiZ averted his gaze. "Now—what about you? Are the holes in your memory starting to fill in?"

"Yes… The haze is clearing," *he* replied, and closed his eyes.

What came to mind was that island… The sea. The sky. Sora and Kairi smiled in his memory.

He sat down in a chair facing DiZ.

"The same thing is happening to everyone who had ties to Sora. Very soon, to them, he'll be like a good friend who was away for a year." DiZ's eye winked as he gave a satisfied smile.

"I've been waiting, and now I want to know. What is it that you want?"

His eye widened again. "Revenge."

He looked at the floor. *He* hadn't expected to hear that word out of DiZ's mouth.

"Now, to wrap things up," DiZ said. "We must dispose of Naminé."

He frowned beneath his hood.

"She did a splendid job with Sora, but it's high time she disappeared. Roxas isn't the only one who was never meant to exist. Take care of it, Ansem."

Making no reply, *he* remained unmoving.

Atop the clock tower, Hayner nibbled at his sea-salt ice cream and watched the setting sun.

"Tomorrow we search the town," he said when he noticed that the others had joined him, but he didn't look away from the sunset.

"The next day is the festival," Pence added, turning back to Roxas and Olette.

"The last day of summer!" Olette said cheerfully.

"Don't remind me! It's already making me sick!" Hayner dramatically rubbed his gut.

"From what I've seen, the culprit for that would be all the ice cream," Pence teased.

Behind him, Roxas was watching his friends. Two more days of summer vacation. Only two days left for them to be together.

Still, they had those two whole days…

"You were never supposed to exist."

That's what Naminé had said to him.

He wasn't supposed to exist? He was Axel's best friend?

My best friends are Hayner, Pence, and Olette, right?

The clock tower bells rang in their enormous clamor. He could hear a train whistle in the distance. Hayner and the others were chatting and laughing.

And yet…it all felt like something happening far away. Roxas gazed at the low sun, still too bright, and tears sprang to his eyes.

Two days left of summer vacation.

—Restoration at 98%—

THE 6th DAY

***THE CITY WAS COVERED IN DARKNESS. THE GLOW OF** the neon signs here and there, in their attempt to alleviate the gloom, made the darkness only deeper. In the dimness, blacker shadows crawled, wriggling up from the ground and taking shape as Heartless.*

They had me surrounded. I held a weapon in each hand—two Keyblades.

As I cut down the Heartless, the thrill of the fight surged through me. I looked up at the dark sky.

There was a boy standing up there on a rooftop, with silver hair and a blindfold covering his eyes. He *appeared to be about the same age as me, but I couldn't be sure. Like me, he wore a black cloak—however, it was clear he wasn't one of us.*

I hurled a Keyblade at him. *But* he *caught it and jumped down the building, toward me. I jumped up to head him off, and in the instant we passed in front of a neon sign, I was sure he could see the face hidden under my hood.*

We both kicked off from the building and landed on the ground at nearly the same time. In the next moment, all the Heartless nearby scattered, and we leaped back to make some distance between us. He *held my Keyblade as if it were perfectly natural. Apparently,* he *could handle a weapon that shouldn't even have stayed in his hand.*

He *rushed at me with the Keyblade.*

The clang of metal on metal sounded, and sparks flew.

We were matched for strength—well, maybe I was a little stronger. Maybe.

With another flurry of sparks, he *fell.*

"Why? Why do you have the Keyblade?!" he *cried.*

That was exactly what I wanted to know.

Why was I born? Why am I here? Why am I fighting you? And how can *you* use a Keyblade, too?

"Shut up!" I shouted...and brought the Keyblade down to finish him.

* * *

Roxas heaved himself up in his bed. That dream hadn't been like the others.

It wasn't Sora and the others...it was me. *I was in the dream myself.*

He climbed out of bed and looked back at the window in time to see a pigeon flap its wings and fly away.

Wondering about the dream, he got dressed and headed out.

Today was the day of the investigation. *Maybe then we'll understand what's behind all these weird things happening to me.*

He checked the clock—it was already past the time he was supposed to meet them. He hopped onto his skateboard and sped over to the hangout.

Once he arrived, he leaned the skateboard against the wall outside, then took a deep breath and went in. The other three were already there, discussing something.

"Man, I could not sleep last night..." Scratching his head, Roxas walked over to join his friends. "Guys...?"

He reached out to tap Hayner's shoulder—and his hand passed right through.

The three of them seemed to be involved in an animated conversation. But even though they moved and acted like they were talking, he couldn't hear their voices.

They saw something and burst out laughing—completely silent.

And then they slipped past him, out of their usual spots.

"What...?" Roxas mumbled.

There was a single photograph resting on the unused water tank they'd been clustered around. It was the picture from in front of the haunted mansion, with Hayner, Pence, Olette—and no Roxas.

He ran outside after them. The low rays of sun streaking into the alley were as dazzling as usual.

But...there were no other people out.

He was about to head for Market Street, when he felt a presence from behind him.

A dark shape appeared, and then someone stepped out from it—Axel.

"Look at what it's come to," Axel said. "I've been given some pretty nasty orders...to destroy you if you refuse to come back with me."

Roxas stared hard at him. What was it Naminé had said...? "We're...best friends, right?"

That was what she'd told him. Roxas didn't have any memories like that himself. *But...we were friends.*

"Well, sure, but I'm not getting turned into a Dusk for— Hey, wait, you remember now?!"

"Um, yeah...," Roxas faltered. It wasn't really true. He didn't *remember* it. Any of it.

"Great!"

Axel looked genuinely happy, very much so. Roxas's chest tightened just a little. But he couldn't let himself worry about that. Axel had just said he was going to destroy Roxas. If he found out that Roxas really didn't remember...he probably would go ahead and do it.

"But, you know, I gotta make sure," Axel went on, his expression still bright. "So, let's see... What's our boss's name?"

Seizing the chance while Axel's guard was down, Roxas picked up a stick from the ground.

"Roxas?" Axel said, anxious now.

Roxas settled into a fighting stance, holding the stick like a sword.

"C'mon, I can't believe this...," Axel muttered.

The stick in Roxas's hand transformed into the Keyblade. "Axel..."

But when Roxas called his name, Axel readied his chakrams. And then—he stopped moving.

He was *paused*, just like before, when Naminé had helped him in the sandlot.

A deep voice spoke from somewhere.

"Roxas. To the mansion. The time has come..."

The mansion? Time for what?

Never mind that... I want to see my friends.

"Hayner...," Roxas called. "Pence..."

But there was no reply.

"Olette...!"

The town was silent. He couldn't hear a sound. In front of him, frozen in time, was his "best friend" Axel.

But Axel was never my best friend. He couldn't have been, or I would remember him.

My friends are the ones who live here, Hayner and Pence and Olette...

He shouted their names again. "Hayner! Pence! Olette!"

His voice echoed in the empty Twilight Town.

"We have intruders," DiZ said.

He stood up and peered at the screen, which showed a map of Twilight Town with glowing dots representing the intruders. And the dots were multiplying.

"That's no good," *he* muttered, gripping a sword that looked like a demon's wing.

"What happened to Naminé?" asked DiZ, just as *he* was heading out.

"She's in her room as usual."

"...And? What about disposing of her?"

He could feel the weight of DiZ's stare on his back. But *he* didn't turn around to reply. "It can still be done. Even after Sora wakes up."

"It is already time. Roxas will be here at the mansion any moment. I don't know what you're scheming... But everything is proceeding in line with my theories."

At that, *he* finally looked at DiZ. "Your objective isn't the same as mine. I hope you don't forget that."

A faint smile came to DiZ's face—or maybe *he* only imagined it.

"When Sora wakes up...this alliance between us is over. Right?"

DiZ glared at *him* wordlessly, never taking his eyes off *his* unhidden face. With a faint smile, *he* left the room.

Time began to move again. Axel heaved an enormous sigh.

Apparently, *they* were still better at playing the situation.

"So the Roxas I know is long gone," Axel mumbled as if to confirm it to himself. "Fine, I see how it is..."

He glowered at the setting sun. Was Roxas really gone?

What could Axel do to find him again?

Soon...Sora would wake up.

How could he separate Sora and Roxas?

"This is bad..." Axel frowned. A dark space yawned behind him, and he vanished into it.

Roxas dashed away to the haunted mansion. Here and there in town those silver creatures, the Dusks, were appearing. Why...? What was happening to Twilight Town?

"Hayner...Pence...Olette..."

Mumbling their names under his breath like a magic spell, he slashed the Keyblade at any Dusks who crossed his path. If he made it through the wall and into the forest, he'd reach the haunted mansion, and there he should be able to find out something.

"Hayner..."

He was always doing ridiculous things with Roxas. They'd fought together in the Struggle, and sometimes they actually quarreled, but they would always make up soon enough.

"Pence..."

Their chowhound friend was kind and thoughtful. He was good with computers, too, always keeping up with what was happening around town and sharing the news.

"Olette..."

She was always smiling. Honest and conscientious, the one who kept the rest of them in line.

He would never believe that those three weren't his friends. He *couldn't* believe it.

And not just them, but Seifer and his gang, too, and everyone in town. All of them—all of them were his friends. He wouldn't think otherwise.

He'd made it through the forest. "Why...?" he murmured as he gazed up at the haunted mansion.

The gate was shut as tight as ever, with its giant lock.

"Don't call me here and then lock me out..."

Behind him Dusks were crowding and jostling, trying to get at him.

Suddenly a memory from those dreams came into his head.

A huge keyhole...and in his hand, the Keyblade.

How had Sora opened these things in the dreams?

Roxas stepped back a bit from the gate and held up the Keyblade, pointing it at the lock. A beam of light shot from the Keyblade—and the gate opened.

"There." Roxas didn't look back once before charging into the mansion.

As the silver things moved to follow Roxas, a man in a black cloak blocked their way.

The gate drew slowly shut at his back, and the Dusks surrounded him. The weapon he held was a sword like a demon's wing—Soul Eater. "Come and get it," he taunted the things.

All at once, they rushed him.

The interior of the mansion was dusty and dim. But why did Roxas feel like he knew this place? Up on the second story, down the hall, there should be...

He rushed through the foyer and up the stairs, taking them two at a stride. The Dusks were still coming after him, but they seemed weak now. When he thought back to the first time he'd fought one of them, he could hardly believe these were the same creatures. The Keyblade felt light in his hand, too.

He couldn't have said whether the difference was in himself or the things around him.

He opened the door at the end of the second-story hall.

"This is..."

Somehow, he'd known what he would find—the white room where he'd talked to Naminé the day before. Drawings covered the walls. Roxas examined them one by one, with the attention he hadn't had the chance to give them yesterday.

Naminé had called herself a witch who could control people's memories.

These drawings pinned to the walls were sketches she'd made of someone's memories—of Sora's and his own.

He paused in front of a certain drawing. Someone dressed in black was running through a dark building.

That's...me.

The moment he realized that, pain shot through his skull.

And his mind went back in time.

I was walking in a dark city lit only by neon signs—the same as the dream I had this morning.

Axel stood there like he'd been waiting for me. I felt my resolve waver when I saw him, but I kept walking.

"Your mind's made up?" he said when I'd passed him by.

I turned back to him. "Why did the Keyblade choose me? I have to know."

There had always been these inexplicable memories in my heart. Things I'd never seen, people I'd never met.

Why was it that I could wield the Keyblade? Why was I separated from Sora? Why did I come into being at all?

I wanted to know.

"You can't turn on the organization!" Axel cried.

He remembered—*I was in the organization.*

Roxas rubbed at his throbbing temples and turned around. Naminé was there, quiet.

"Organization XIII... They're a bad bunch," he said, as if to tell himself.

Naminé shook her head and looked at the floor as she spoke. "Bad or good—I don't know. They're a group of incomplete people who want to be whole. And to that end, they're searching desperately for something."

"What?" Roxas asked.

She raised her eyes to him and took a tiny breath. "Kingdom Hearts."

"...Kingdom...Hearts?" He couldn't stifle a smile as he repeated the words.

"Funny?" Naminé questioned his reaction.

"No, it's just..." Roxas took a step toward her, shaking his head. "I think I've been running away from the question I really wanna ask. What's going to happen to me? Just tell me that. Nothing else really matters anymore."

He just wanted to know. *What's going to happen to me? Why did all this happen?*

Hayner, Pence, Olette. Sora, Donald, Goofy...and Naminé, and Axel, the man in black.

People he knew, and people he didn't. But maybe he did know the people he didn't know. Maybe he didn't know the people he did know.

He wasn't even sure which was which anymore.

"You are...," Naminé began—but then she flickered and vanished, like some kind of mirage.

"Naminé?"

Roxas dashed to the space where she'd been standing, and a man appeared there in a flash of light.

The man in red. The one who appeared when Axel was talking to me, the day of the Struggle...

The Dusks appeared as quickly as they were defeated, but *he* kept on cutting down the silver creatures.

Then a scream pierced the air. "Help! Please!"

He turned. It sounded like someone *he* knew—like *her.*

But it was Naminé standing in front of the gate. In that instant, there was no doubt whose Nobody she was.

"Please, don't let them hurt Roxas anymore!" She clung desperately to his back. "We Nobodies were never supposed to exist. But this...it's horrible!"

He lowered Soul Eater and held her close.

A voice spoke from among the Dusks. "So, is Roxas inside?"

"Axel...," Naminé murmured.

He looked up to find a red-haired man standing there. Probably a member of the organization. *He* lifted Soul Eater again. "Who are you?" he growled.

Axel only readied his chakrams in reply.

Naminé spoke up into the tension. "Axel... He's Roxas's friend. A Nobody. And a member of the organization... But he—"

Axel smirked and cut her off. "Let me tell you something, Naminé—you and I both want the same thing. Got it memorized?"

Naminé shook her head. "It's the same...and it isn't. But I don't have time to explain."

Listening to them, *he* glared hard at Axel.

"I'm sorry, Axel." Just as Naminé spoke, a black portal opened up behind her and *him*. It swallowed them, and then they were gone.

"Hey—what gives?!" Axel ran to the empty space. Nothing was there but the gate locked tight, barring his way. He clicked his tongue in frustration and stared up at the looming mansion.

* * *

The man in the red cape spoke at a measured pace. "There is no knowledge that has the power to change your fate."

"Even if it doesn't...I still want to know. I have the right to know," Roxas said, his voice hushed.

No matter what, he wanted to understand what his fate was... what was going to happen to him.

"A Nobody has no rights. Not even the right to exist."

"But what *is* a Nobody?!" shouted Roxas, losing his cool, and then the man in the black cloak appeared between them from a dark portal.

"DiZ, we're out of time. The Dusks are everywhere!"

As if following the sound of his cry, another dark portal materialized behind DiZ.

"Roxas..." It was Naminé who stepped out of it, now loud and urgent. "Nobodies like us are only half a person. You won't disappear. You'll be whole again!"

"I'm going to...disappear?" Roxas said.

DiZ turned and seized Naminé by the arm. "No more of this mutiny!"

"No, you won't disappear! You'll—" Naminé began to tell Roxas, but DiZ clamped a hand over her mouth and pulled her with him toward the portal.

"Hey, wait!" Roxas ran to them, or tried to—the man in the black cloak was in his way.

Struggling with all her might, Naminé wriggled away from DiZ's suffocating hand and raised her voice. "Roxas! We'll meet again! And then we can talk about everything. I may not know it's you, and you may not know it's me—but we will meet again! I promise—I know we will!"

"No! Wait!" Roxas tried to get to them, but before his eyes, Naminé vanished, dragged into the dark. "Naminé!"

The dark portal closed up, and the man in the black cloak disappeared, too.

"What…what just happened…?" Roxas mumbled, stunned. And then he yelled, "What's going *on*?!"

He flung his arm out in frustration and hit a chair, and a single drawing fell from the jostled table.

It was a picture of Roxas and Sora holding hands.

DiZ released Naminé's arm and shoved her away. She fell to the floor of the computer room.

On the screen there was an image of Sora.

"To think a mere Nobody would act so selfishly…," DiZ grumbled under his breath.

Meanwhile, *he* helped Naminé to her feet.

"Why…were Nobodies born? Why did we have to exist at all? You know the answers, don't you?" Naminé demanded, holding *his* hand as she pulled herself up.

"I bear no obligation to give them to you," DiZ replied without looking at her.

"Don't you remember? I'm a witch."

He burst out laughing at her and spun around, his cape fluttering behind him. "You think you can compel me? Didn't you make a 'promise' to Sora and Riku?"

"I didn't promise *you* anything," Naminé retorted.

She hadn't. Naminé had not made any promises to DiZ.

The promise I made was…

"I shall tell you one more thing," DiZ said. "If you hadn't gone to such lengths in the first place, Roxas would not be in so much pain. Isn't that so?"

"Knowing something painful is still better than not knowing. Being able to help someone is better, even if it hurts. I have no memories at all. I don't know anything, just like the Replica. So I want to know. Roxas is the same way."

"And what good will that do you?!"

Just as DiZ shot down her argument, *he* noticed that behind him the screen was alerting them to something. Naminé did, too.

An intruder in the mansion—most likely Axel.

"What *do* you know, DiZ?" Naminé demanded.

When *he* realized what she was doing, he instinctively sensed that he shouldn't inform DiZ.

She kept interrogating him. "What are you trying to do?"

"Revenge," *he* replied, even before DiZ could answer her.

Behind DiZ, the screen told them that Roxas had infiltrated the computer room in the simulated mansion. And Axel was lying in wait for him.

Axel, Roxas's best friend... He'd said that he and Naminé both wanted the same thing.

The same and not the same, she'd told him.

If *he* were in Axel's place, he wouldn't be able to destroy Roxas. *He* knew that much.

That meant they were buying Roxas time right now. It shouldn't cause any problems.

"This old man is using us just to get his own personal revenge," *he* said. "Isn't that right?"

"Do you really intend to betray me, Ansem?" DiZ's voice shook with anger.

But then, DiZ reflected, if Ansem was going to betray him...it wouldn't be the first time.

On the second story of the mansion, in a room opposite from the white room Naminé had occupied, Roxas was running down a hidden staircase that led down to the basement.

There was only one thing he knew. *They led me here, and now I have to keep going. Even if I turn back, I won't regain anything that's important to me.*

Beyond the basement door, there was an enormous computer setup.

The monitor showed an image of Sora. The headache came back—more memories were returning.

"Shut up!"

I brought down the Keyblade—and darkness surged from him, *unbelievably strong.*

He *was on his feet again, and he looked like someone else.*

But I didn't have the chance to see who. The fierce rush of darkness threw me back.

And then he *brought me into the computer room in the basement.*

My head was pounding, and I could hear two people talking.

"Will it work?" asked the man in the black coat, the one who defeated me.

"If we can maintain the simulated town until Naminé finishes chaining together Sora's memories." That was the man in the red cape.

"What'll happen to Roxas?"

"He holds half of Sora's power within him. In the end, he'll have to give it back. Until then, he'll need another personality to throw off his pursuers."

Another personality? Did I become someone else?

"Simulated town"? Is that Twilight Town?

Then what about Hayner, Pence, and Olette?

"Poor thing...," murmured the man in black.

"It's only a Nobody," said the one in red.

Only a Nobody?

What is a Nobody?!

The memory that returned so painfully to his head was a horribly unwelcome truth.

In Roxas's hand, the Keyblade shone.

He winced, holding back the tears stinging his eyes, and struck out at the computer with the Keyblade, over and over.

All his memories were fake—and not just his memories. His friends, even the town—everything. It was all fake.

How…?

Roxas stared at the smashed computer.

Then, behind him, a door opened. He ran to it, and Axel was waiting. Roxas mumbled his name.

"You really do remember me this time? I'm *flattered*!" A mean, twisted smile came to Axel's face as he conjured his chakrams.

I really don't, though, Roxas thought. *And I don't know why you're following me.*

Naminé had said Axel was his best friend. Then why was Axel trying to destroy him?

But more than that—everything about his situation was so disgusting. He was so upset it made him sick.

"Too late, though!" Axel yelled. Flames erupted in the air around him.

If Axel wants to destroy me… Fine! He can try!

The moment Roxas felt the power coursing into him, with a flash of light a Keyblade appeared in each of his hands.

"*Two?!*" Axel fumed and rushed in to attack, but Roxas crossed the Keyblades and blocked. "Huh. Not bad, *Roxas*…"

Axel grinned, and then another memory came flooding back.

In that city lit only by neon lights, Axel shouted at me. "You get on their bad side, and they'll destroy you!"

This happened right after the memory that came to me in the white room.

"No one would miss me," I retorted, and started to walk away.

"That's not true…," Axel mumbled. "I would."

At the time, I pretended not to hear him.

We Nobodies have no hearts. How would we be able to "miss" someone?

But now, I understand how he felt.

Roxas flung Axel back with the Keyblades so that he fell to his knees.

Roxas couldn't bring himself to deal the final blow. "Axel…"

That's right—we were the only pair of best friends in the organization.

"Let's meet again in the next life." A dark mist rose around Axel as he spoke.

"Yeah. I'll be waiting."

"Silly. Just because you have a next life..."

Axel was breathing hard, his shoulders heaving, as the darkness swallowed him up. Roxas didn't look away until well after he disappeared.

A train pulled sedately into Twilight Town—the ghost train, decorated violet. The passenger who disembarked wore a black cloak like the organization members. He was fairly short, and the hood of his cloak couldn't quite hide his two big ears.

King Mickey hopped swiftly down the stairs from the platform and dashed out into town.

As DiZ trembled with rage, *he* answered quietly. "No, I'm not betraying you. You said our alliance would hold until Sora wakes up. Well, that's about to happen. Everything until then is up to you. But after that, I...*we* can take care of things on our own."

He had no intention of getting involved in someone else's revenge plot.

Besides, *he* wanted to help Naminé, who was *her* Nobody, and Roxas, who was Sora's Nobody. What her Nobody wanted was probably the same as what she herself wanted. What Sora's Nobody wanted was probably the same as what Sora himself wanted.

Were Nobodies really not supposed to exist...? Did that mean none of them could be allowed to exist?

It was like the duality of light and darkness.

The worlds weren't made only of light—and darkness wasn't always evil. *I found those answers for myself.*

And even if Nobodies weren't supposed to exist, that didn't mean it was okay to hurt them.

Naminé called *him* by his name. "......Riku."

"I'm not Riku," he said. "I'm Ansem. Let's go, Naminé."

Riku took Naminé by the hand and made to leave.

"Where?" she asked uncertainly.

I'm a Nobody, she thought. *Where could I possibly go...?*

"Well...it looks like someone's here to tell us," Riku said.

"Huh?" Naminé could sense that Riku was smiling under his hood, and she looked up at him.

"You, make sure Sora wakes up properly," he told DiZ. "Look at the screen. Roxas is about to reach the room where Sora is. Weren't you planning to leave the rest to Sora himself?"

He didn't know what had happened between Roxas and Axel, but they'd been right not to interfere with it. Roxas heading for the pod room told them that much.

DiZ laughed softly.

Riku didn't like it. "What's so funny?"

"Oh—nothing. I'll go and meet Roxas." With those parting words, DiZ vanished.

"Come on, Naminé," Riku said, squeezing her hand.

"...Okay."

The reality is harsh, he thought. *But still...we have to keep going.*

Riku and Naminé left the room in silence.

This place looked like the room where Naminé had been. White walls, white ceiling, even a white floor.

In the middle of that floor was some kind of pod shaped like a flower bud. And in front of it, the man in the red cape stood silently.

"At last," DiZ said. "The Keyblade's chosen one."

"Who are you talking to?" Roxas snapped, glaring at him. "Me or Sora?"

"To half of Sora, of course. You reside in darkness. What I need is someone who can move about the realm of light and destroy Organization XIII." DiZ's voice was a low rumble.

"Why? Who are you?"

"I am a servant of the world. And if I'm a servant, you are at best a tool." As if his own words amused him, DiZ started to chuckle.

"Was…was that supposed to be a joke? 'Cos I'm not laughing!" Roxas lunged at DiZ, swinging the Keyblade, but it passed right through him with no impact.

"Sorry to disappoint," DiZ said, "but this is only a projection made of data."

Roxas screamed in wordless fury.

Sorrow…rage…hate. What was he supposed to do with these feelings?

The best he could do was to hack wildly at DiZ with the Keyblade. Even if it was just an illusion, he had to take out those feelings on it or else he would explode.

"Over here." DiZ vanished and reappeared, his back up against the pod, looking down at Roxas.

"I—I hate you so much…," Roxas spat.

"You should share some of that hatred with Sora. He's far too kind."

"No! My heart belongs to me!" Roxas brought the Keyblade down on him—but DiZ vanished again, and the Keyblade struck the pod.

"…Huh?"

The petals came quietly open.

"Sora…"

Sora floated inside the pod like a cloud, his eyes closed.

My other half… My—

The boy sleeping there wasn't a dream. He was real.

"I'm jealous…," Roxas murmured. Sora looked so peaceful, it made him sad.

He stepped closer to the boy in the pod.

"Looks like my summer vacation…is over."

As he spoke softly, light engulfed them.

A sweet, peaceful light. A light that was complete.

"Sora…"

At Roxas's whisper, he awoke.

CHAPTER 7

THE LAST DAY

SOMEONE WAS CALLING HIM.

Who…?

Who was saying his name?

"Sora!"

"Sora, wake up!"

The voices were familiar. He blinked his eyes open, and in front of him were Donald and Goofy.

Sora took a moment to stretch and then lazily jumped out of the pod, where he hugged the two waiting to see him. "Donald! Goofy!"

They all embraced and then kept their hands linked, so glad to be reunited.

"Goodness, that was some nap!" Jiminy Cricket poked out of Sora's hood and hopped down to the floor.

"You mean we were asleep?" Sora said.

Jiminy cocked his little head. "I think we must've been. Or we wouldn't be so drowsy…"

"When do ya think we went to sleep?" Goofy wondered. Sora was confused, too.

When did *we fall asleep? What were we doing before that?* He couldn't quite remember.

"Let's see," Sora thought aloud. "We defeated Ansem, right?"

"Yup." Goofy nodded.

"Restored peace to the world… Found Kairi… Oh yeah—and then we went to look for Riku."

"Then what?" Donald said.

"And then…," Sora started. "Um, and then… Hmm."

The four of them sank into thought.

It was fair to say they really had no memory of what had happened after that.

"What's your journal say, Jiminy?" Goofy asked.

If it had happened on their journey, Jiminy would have written it down.

"Gee, there's only one sentence," Jiminy told them.

The others peered at the tiny journal. It was cricket-sized, and the letters were too small for them to read, but they could see that there was indeed just one short sentence on the page.

"'Thank Naminé'...," Jiminy read. "Hmm. I wonder who that is."

Sora, Donald, and Goofy looked at one another. *Naminé...* They couldn't remember hearing a name like that.

"Welp, if we meet any Naminés, then we gotta tell 'em thanks."

Sora nodded to Goofy's sensible statement.

"For now, why don't we go outside and see where we are?" Jiminy suggested, and sprang back up to Sora's shoulder.

Donald and Goofy checked their effects—Donald's wand and Goofy's shield—and began looking for a way out.

The floor, the ceiling, the walls were all white, and at one end of the room there was a grand door. When they opened it, brilliant light streamed in...and outside was a mansion's spacious garden, dotted with crumbling stone pillars.

"What's this place supposed to be?" Donald said, squinting in the sunlight.

"Dunno, but it's kinda excitin'." Goofy looked around with intense curiosity.

They went through the garden to a massive gate that had been left open, and beyond that was a gloomy forest.

Sora hung back nervously. "It's pretty dark up ahead..."

"Should we go back to the mansion?" Goofy asked.

"You turn into a fraidycat while you were asleep, Sora?" Donald teased.

"Yeah, right! C'mon, let's go! Donald! Goofy!" Sora charged into the woods.

Donald hid behind him. "Looks like something's gonna come out at us..."

"Look who's the fraidycat now," Sora said, laughing.

And yet, this forest... Not only the forest. The garden, too. They felt vaguely familiar. *Have I been here before?* Sora wondered.

"There's light up thataway!" Goofy ran toward it, with Sora and Donald close behind him.

Axel stared vacantly at the sun sinking into the sea.

The never-ending sound of the waves was beginning to grate on him. He was far outside Twilight Town, as far as the trains went, at a deserted beach. It was the same beach Roxas and his friends had meant to visit.

He stood up from the hunk of driftwood he'd perched on and flinched as pain shot through his ribs. "Ouuuch… He could've gone a *little* easier on me…"

Axel still hadn't quite healed from his fight with Roxas. He sat himself back down on the driftwood, resting his elbows on his knees, and watched the waves rush in and out.

He wasn't sure what to do yet. He would already be branded a traitor. He hadn't exactly disobeyed orders…but he had failed to carry them out.

The other members were already suspicious of him as the lone survivor from Castle Oblivion. He couldn't imagine that it was safe for him to return to the organization.

"Oh man, what do I do…?" He stretched carefully and got up again, his eyes narrowed against the setting sun. It turned the sea red, and the sky. The waves lapped at his feet, getting them wet.

"Axel," said a voice from behind him.

Startled, he turned. It was…

"Naminé…"

He stiffened warily, but she only gave him an awkward smile.

And there was a man standing behind her. He wore the same black cloak, but he wasn't in the organization—Axel knew that much. He had a feeling it was the man he'd met outside the mansion.

Forcing his injured body to move, Axel readied his chakrams.

"Axel, don't…" Naminé looked back at the other man, whose

empty hands were resting at his sides, trying to show that he wasn't an enemy.

Axel sucked in a breath and sat down once more on the hunk of driftwood. "So, what's your name?"

"...Ansem."

"*Ansem?* Somehow I doubt that."

Ansem—or rather, Riku—shrugged off the question. "Never mind my name. I want to offer you a bargain."

Axel pretended that this didn't rattle him as he stared back at Riku.

Through the forest, there was a town built mostly of brick.

"There's people here! We can ask somebody where we are." Donald ran toward them to ask.

Watching him, Sora cocked his head. "Hmm..."

"What's the matter, Sora?" Goofy asked, concerned.

"You know...I think I've been to this town."

He didn't know why, but he felt it—something in him knew this place.

"*Quack!* Sora! It's called Twilight Town!" Donald shouted back to them.

Twilight Town... That name was familiar, too.

Just then, the toll of enormous bells sounded through the town.

"Gawrsh, those sure are some bells," Goofy remarked. "Reminds me of Traverse Town."

That town had a huge bell, too...

"Oh. I guess...," Sora said absently, concentrating. "Actually, I think I know somewhere we need to go."

Somewhere he had to go... Somewhere he usually went. He thought he remembered something like that. He broke into a run.

"Hey, Sora, where ya goin'?" Goofy called, chasing after him.

"C'mon! This way!"

"*Wak!*" Donald, listening to the people tell him about Twilight Town, jumped to follow them.

Up this slope and then into this alley… And then…

"Wait up, Sora!" Goofy was panting and wheezing.

"Don't just take off like that!" Donald scolded, bringing up the rear with a scowl.

"Hmm… It's here." Sora zeroed in on the fenced-off corner of the alley.

"What's here?" Donald pushed open the fence and stepped in without hesitating, his webbed feet slapping the ground.

"Hey, what d'you want?!" an angry voice yelled. Sora and Goofy exchanged glances and ran in after Donald.

Scratching his head, Sora grasped for an excuse. "Uh, nothing… Just thought something might be back here…"

Past the fence there were two boys and one girl, all about the same age as him.

"Now you know," snapped a boy with spiky hair, who occupied the highest space he could sit in. "This is *our* spot."

"Um…," the heavyset boy began, looking puzzled, and he walked up to Sora to peer into his face.

"What?"

"We've…never met before, right? I'm Pence." He grinned brightly.

The other boy seemed to give in and jumped down from his vantage point. The girl got up from her seat on a wooden crate.

"I'm Hayner," said the spiky-haired boy. "It's good to meet you, but we got stuff to do, so catch ya later." He headed out to the fence.

"My name's Olette," said the girl, introducing herself warmly. "Hey, did you finish up the summer homework yet? These projects are just the worst, huh?"

"Homework?" Sora blurted, a bit bewildered.

"Hey, what're your names?" Pence asked.

Sora exchanged glances with his friends.

Unruffled, Goofy spoke up. "We're Sora and Donald and Goofy."

"Hi," Sora added, holding out a hand to shake, but Pence and Olette just looked at each other.

"Sora and Donald and Goofy... We just met someone who's looking for you," Olette said.

Now the trio looked at one another again.

"Sure looked like he was in a hurry," Pence said. "He was wearing a black cloak, and I couldn't see his face, but he had these big round ears."

"The king!" Donald exclaimed, jumping up.

"Where'd you see him?" asked Sora.

"The station."

"The station! Thanks!" Sora nodded at the other two. *The king is looking for us!*

"Well, we'd better get back to that assignment!" Olette started for the fence, too.

"See you." Pence followed her out.

"Okay, let's head to the station!" Sora said, and the other two nodded.

They dashed outside—or started to—but then Goofy stopped short in his tracks, and Sora and Donald ran right into him.

"What'dja do that for?" Sora complained.

Goofy slowly turned to look at him. "Uh...which way's the station?"

"Oh—it's this way!" Sora ran up the hill.

"*Wak!* Stop running off!" Donald tried to keep up.

"Sora? How d'you know?" Goofy said.

"I just do!" Sora called back over his shoulder.

It was true. Somehow, he just knew this town. Up atop the hill, they would find the plaza in front of the station.

"Is that it?" Goofy asked.

Sora paused and then walked up to the building. "Probably."

"Your Majesty?" Donald called.

"Maybe he's not here," Goofy said, perplexed—and then they found themselves surrounded by silver creatures of a sort none of them had ever seen before. "*Yipe!*"

"H-Heartless?!" Donald gripped his wand.

"No—these aren't Heartless!" Sora rushed at the squirming silver things. In the next second he had the shining Keyblade in his hand, and he brought it down on them as they tried to wriggle away.

"Fire!"

"Here goes!"

Donald waved his wand as Goofy swatted the things with his shield.

But no matter how many they defeated, more enemies appeared to surround them again.

"They just keep comin'!"

Just as Donald shouted, a shadowy black figure came to scatter the creatures.

The newcomer was smaller than Sora by a foot—no, by two. He held a Keyblade, and his hood didn't quite hide a pair of big ears.

Sora was leaning closer to make sure he was really seeing what he thought he saw, and then, noticing the ears, Donald and Goofy practically climbed atop him. This resulted in the three of them falling flat, with Sora on the bottom, but they hardly noticed as they exclaimed in unison, "Your Majesty?!"

"Shh!" King Mickey turned to glance at them, a finger to his lips. "You gotta board the train and leave town. The train knows the way. Here, take this."

In his hand was a cute little cloth purse. Sora took it and examined it closely. It was much heavier than it looked—probably because it was stuffed full of munny.

"Your Majesty?" Donald said tentatively, but King Mickey was already dashing away across the plaza.

"The king…," Sora mumbled, still staring at the purse. "Was that really him?"

"It coulda been… Yep, I know it was!" Goofy was facing the direction where King Mickey had disappeared.

Donald hopped happily in place. "Now we know he's okay!"

"The king was locked in the realm of darkness with Riku, wasn't he?" Sora said. "But we just saw him..."

"Yep." Donald nodded.

Sora brightened. "So if the king is here, that means Riku is around somewhere!"

"He's gotta be!" Donald agreed forcefully.

"I'm gonna look for Riku. Then we can go back to our islands together. Kairi's there waiting for us! What are you two gonna do?"

"Gawrsh, Sora..." Goofy sounded disapproving. "Do ya have to ask?"

Seeing his face, Sora laughed.

"What's so funny?!" Donald scolded.

"Your faces!"

Donald and Goofy looked at each other. Their faces were pretty funny. The three of them burst out laughing together.

"What d'ya say, guys?" Sora said, determined, when they recovered. "Let's stick together for another journey."

Donald and Goofy nodded.

If the train knows where to take us like the king said, Riku has to be there, Sora thought. Sora had to go to Riku...and then home to the islands, where Kairi was.

"Let's go!" Sora ran up the steps to the station, and he was heading to the platform, when someone called to them.

"Wait up!"

"...Hayner?" Sora looked back to find Hayner and Pence and Olette waiting at the bottom of the stairs to the platform.

Finally Hayner stepped closer, struggling to say what he wanted to. "Hey, Sora..."

"What?"

"It's nothing, but..." Hayner looked at the floor. Whatever he was having trouble saying, it seemed important.

Pence picked up the thread. "We came to see you off. It just seemed like something we oughta do."

"Oh…really?" Sora said. "Thanks!"

Just as that word was out of his mouth, the signal bell on the platform rang.

"You should hurry and get your tickets," Olette reminded him.

Sora ran to the ticket window and reached into his pocket for the purse full of munny that King Mickey had given to him.

"Huh?" Seeing the purse, Olette cocked her head.

"What is it?" asked Donald.

In response, Olette took a small purse from her own pocket. It was identical to the one Sora held, embroidery and all.

"They're the same," Goofy remarked.

"Yeah." Olette nodded, a little mystified.

"Three tickets, please," Sora said at the ticket window. As he took some coins from the purse, a piece of paper and a little blue crystal ball fell to the floor. "Hey… What's this?"

"More treasures for us to share."

Those words came up from somewhere deep in his heart when he looked at the crystal.

Who had said that?

"Sora, hurry up!" Donald called, jumping up the stairs to the platform.

"Uh-huh…" Sora put the slip of paper back in the purse and pocketed the crystal.

Goofy was calling to him, too. "What's the matter, Sora? C'mon!"

"It's just…I can't help feeling like we won't see this town again." A sense of separation was coming over him for some reason.

"Aw, you're thinkin' too much," Goofy told him, easygoing as ever.

"Yeah… You're right." Sora plodded up the steps to the platform. Somehow, he felt…incredibly sad.

"Sora! Move it!" Donald was waiting by the train doors.

Hayner and his friends were climbing the steps behind Sora. And…they looked sad, too.

Sora had just begun to shake it off, his mind made up. "Okay, let's go!"

Donald and Goofy nodded and jumped into the train car.

"Bye!" Sora turned back to Hayner and his friends and forced himself to smile for them.

"Hey, Sora… You sure we haven't met before?" Hayner said, with Pence and Olette staring at him, a little surprised.

"Pretty sure…," Sora replied, but his head was cocked uncertainly. "Why?"

He couldn't have met Hayner and the others before.

But then…why am I so sad to leave them now?

"Heh… I dunno." Hayner smiled awkwardly.

Tears welled up in Sora's eyes and a drop spilled down his cheek. "Huh…?"

He had no idea why he would be crying. He rushed to wipe it away.

He was sad but happy. Happy and yet sad…

"You okay?" Worried, Olette peered at him closely.

"Y-yeah. Don't know where that came from." The tears had already stopped.

"Pull it together," Hayner said, covering with mock exasperation.

"Right… See you."

Hayner, Pence, and Olette followed Sora as far as the train door. He didn't know what to say to them, and he just waved, then climbed aboard. As they watched, the doors closed with a *thunk*.

The train smoothly began to pull out. Sora could see the trio on the platform, staring at the train—watching him quietly, not even waving to him.

The purse from King Mickey was in his pocket along with that little crystal.

"You know…," Sora murmured. Donald and Goofy stopped looking out the windows and turned to him. "This…hurts."

He clutched the crystal in his pocket. Something in his chest ached. He didn't know why he felt like this.

"We'll come back," Donald told him with a shrug.

"Yeah," Goofy added. "We can visit Hayner and those guys again."

"You're right."

As Sora nodded to them, the train rolled out into the light, taking them onward to a new journey.

WILL THE DAY COME WHEN THIS BATTLE, BORN OF *confusion, shall end?*

It is different things to different people.

Can the reality be that which is hidden?

The reason is simply existence itself.
Still, memories can be trusted.

Be not afraid. Give yourself over to the sound of the waves.
By and by, your fleeting rest will come to an end…

And everything will begin.

THE DESTRUCTION OF HOLLOW BASTION

PROLOGUE

AND ALONE...

SENSING THAT SORA AND HIS FRIENDS HAD SET OUT on their journey, Naminé opened her eyes. Her hands, clasped as if in prayer, fell to her sides, and she lifted her gaze to the man in the black cloak beside her.

"So we're leaving, too?" said Ansem—who was actually Riku.

They were on a quiet beach not too far from Twilight Town.

"Do you two even have anywhere to go?" Axel wondered from his perch on one of the boulders that dotted the shore.

"Do *you*?" Riku replied, staring out at the horizon.

"I never had anywhere to go in the first place. We Nobodies don't belong, period. Nowhere to go and nowhere to come home to. Right, Naminé?"

She didn't answer, but only looked down at the sand.

He's right. We Nobodies don't know why we were born or where we should go.

"The bargain's over now," Riku said to Naminé's back. "We don't have to listen to that guy anymore, do we?" He sounded as if he wanted to confirm it with her.

"Well...," Naminé faltered, unable to raise her eyes.

What was she supposed to do now?

Should she go with Riku? Should she part ways with Axel?

Riku and I are different, she thought. *But Axel and I are...the same.*

As if he had picked up on her hesitation, Axel stood and stretched. "I'm gonna have to go a different direction. You and me, we don't want the same thing. Just like you and DiZ didn't. I don't know about Naminé, though."

Riku winced momentarily at his words.

"I...I want to help Sora and his friends," Naminé said, eyes still downcast, but determination audible in her voice.

"Well then, that guy right there behind you is gonna get rid of you," Axel remarked. "Just like he did to Roxas."

Naminé whirled toward Riku. "DiZ...told you to eliminate me?"

Riku didn't move.

"He did, didn't he...?" she demanded again, and finally Riku gave her a tiny nod. "So, I really shouldn't go with you."

"...That's not true."

Naminé shook her head.

"Let's go, Naminé," Axel called to her.

Without a word, she nodded to Axel, and behind them, a dark portal opened up.

"Where are you going?" Riku clenched his fists to keep from reaching out for her.

"I don't know... But we'll meet again, Riku." She smiled at him.

"...Is that a promise?" Riku asked hesitantly.

She dipped her head once. "Yes. A promise. We might go separate ways for now, but we'll see each other again. Won't we?"

"Okay. I promise." Riku nodded more forcefully.

And then Naminé and Axel vanished into the dark portal.

"I'm sorry, Riku," she told him softly, but the whisper never reached him.

Alone on the beach, all Riku could hear was the sound of the waves, sending his memory back to the island.

CHAPTER 1
MYSTERIOUS TOWER

THE TRAIN QUIETLY CAME TO A HALT.

"...Is this the last stop?" Donald cocked his head at the view from the window.

"Kind of a funny-lookin' place," Goofy noted with an anxious glance toward Sora.

A light fog obscured the scene outside the train, making it hard to tell what sort of place they'd found themselves in. They only knew there was land.

"Let's go," Sora said. The other two nodded.

When they approached the door, it slid open for them as if it knew, and they stepped tentatively off the train.

"Have ya ever seen this place before?" Goofy's head swiveled from side to side.

Donald was doing the same. "Nope."

The "land" seemed to be an island floating in the air.

"This has to be where King Mickey told us to go. C'mon!" Sora dashed ahead.

"Sora, wait up!" Donald tried to chase after him but fell flat on his bill.

"Did you forget how to run after sleeping so long?" Sora teased over his shoulder.

Donald hopped up with an indignant "*Quack!*" and stomped furiously toward Sora. "That's enough outta you!"

But Sora was focused on the train behind him, perplexed.

"Sora!" Donald huffed.

The boy didn't move.

"Hello? Sora?" Goofy finally joined them.

Sora quietly pointed to the train—or rather, where the train had been. "It's gone..."

"*Wak?!*" Donald started. There was nothing but empty air. Even the railroad was gone.

"Guess we just have to keep going," Sora said.

"Yup, guess so," Goofy agreed, sounding unconcerned, apparently more interested in the middle of the island. "Look, there's a building."

Sora and Donald followed his line of sight to a tall tower stretching up toward the night sky.

"You think anyone's there?" Goofy asked.

"Only one way to find out!" Sora dashed ahead yet again.

The high-pitched rip of fabric soon followed.

"Huh?" The boy searched his clothes for the tear.

"You got a rip here," Goofy said, peering at his side, under his arm.

Sora wouldn't have noticed on his own, but apparently he had grown quite a bit during the year he'd been asleep. The Keyblade wielder's pants barely reached his knees now, so that they served more as shorts.

"Gawrsh, Sora, you're sure growin' fast." Goofy nodded, impressed.

Donald agreed, but added, "Still pretty short, though."

"Hey, what's that supposed to mean?" Sora scowled.

Another noise interrupted them—this time something strange from the tower.

"Didja hear that?" Goofy cupped his hand to his perked ear, his head tilted.

"Sure did!" Sora ran toward the source of the noise.

A bulky armored shape was peeking inside the tower through the gap between the double doors. At first glance, there didn't seem to be much cause for suspicion.

"Whatcha doin'?" asked Donald.

The figure replied without sparing a glance, "Heh-heh. I sent some of my lackeys inside to see if the master of this here tower's as big and tough as they say. Word is he's a real powerful sorcerer. Which would make him the perfect bodyguard for me."

The haughty voice belonged to a male. The trio exchanged glances.

"See, it don't matter how tough he is," he went on. "Once he's a Heartless, he'll do what I say!"

Donald leaped up at the familiar term. "A Heartless?"

Sora and Goofy tensed, prepared for a fight.

"That's right! Those things that come outta the darkness in folks' hearts. And with all those Heartless at her side, Maleficent's gonna conquer everything! And since I got me a debt to pay to that nice ol' witch, I'm goin' round to a bunch of different worlds, buildin' an army of Heartless, special for her. Get it?" He waved his arms as if lecturing them, even though he never took his eyes off the gap into the tower. "Why am I talkin' to you pip-squeaks, anyway? Go on, scram! I'm behind schedule already!"

He shooed them away once more.

"You oughta find something nicer to do," Goofy said.

And the trio had soundly defeated Maleficent, hadn't they?

"Says who?" The person at the door finally turned to face them. "Wha—? *Aaaugh!* It's you!"

At the same time, Donald and Goofy leaped back, also startled, and shouted, "Pete!"

So that was the name of the guy at the door.

"What are you two nimrods doin' here?!"

"What're *you* doing?!" Donald retorted.

"Uh… Friend of yours?" Sora whispered to Goofy, finally catching on.

"Pete used to cause trouble all the time in our world. His Majesty banished him to another dimension a long time ago. Wonder how he escaped…?" Goofy folded his arms in thought.

Pete burst into loud, mean laughter. "You wanna know how, eh? Maleficent busted me out, that's how! And now your world—nah, all the worlds are gonna belong to yours truly!" he announced in one blustery breath, enormously full of himself, then made a small amendment: "And Maleficent, of course."

The trio exchanged dubious grins.

"Maleficent, huh?" Sora remarked.

"What's so funny?!" Any moment now, steam would come pouring from Pete's ears, or so it seemed. "Why, Maleficent's power is so great—"

Sora cut him off. "She's gone."

"Huh?"

"Maleficent won't be helpin' ya now," Goofy said breezily.

"Whaddaya mean?!" Pete bellowed, red-faced.

Donald clamped his bill shut to contain his laughter.

"You!" As Pete finally deduced the situation, he started trembling with rage. "So *you're* the ones that did it!"

"Well..." Sora shrugged as if confessing to a bout of mischief. "We might've had something to do with it."

Pete snarled, staring at his feet and shaking as he tried to contain himself. The trio exchanged a glance, wondering what to do, but at last Pete shouted again. "Heartless squad! Round up!"

On cue, Heartless rose from the ground.

"Whoa!" Gripping his wand, Donald jumped away from one that appeared right beside him.

"Actually...this'll be kinda fun!" Sora rubbed his nose in anticipation and readied the Keyblade.

"Gawrsh, Sora, I sure wouldn't!" Goofy said, sounding a bit confused.

The ring of Heartless crept closer and closer.

"This won't even take a second!" Sora hurtled at them.

A ball of flame shot from Donald's wand. *"Fire!"*

"Aw, shucks... *Yahoooey!*" Goofy rushed at the Heartless on the other side.

Sure enough, scarcely a second later, the Heartless were gone.

Sora grinned at Pete. "Wanna keep going?"

"You just wait! Nobody, and I mean *nobody*, messes with the mighty Pete!" The trembling had turned to violent shaking.

"So, 'mighty' Pete, who lives in this tower anyway?" Sora asked casually, his hands linked behind his head.

"Oh, ya don't know, huh? It's old Yen Sid. 'Course, he's probably a Heartless by now!" Pete sneered.

Hearing the name, Donald hopped in surprise. "Master Yen Sid is *here*?!"

He shoved Pete out of the way, yanked the doors open, and then waddled hastily into the tower.

"Yen Sid? Who's that?" Sora asked Goofy, mystified.

"He's the king's teacher!" Goofy replied, halfway into the tower himself.

"Wow. He must be powerful!" The last of the three followed them.

"Hey! Hold it right there, pip-squeaks!" Pete started to run after the trio, but the doors slammed in his face with a *boom* and enough force to send him tumbling backward. "You won't get away with this!"

But inside the tower, Sora and his friends never even heard Pete's blustering.

Amid the soft rush of the waves, he idled on the seashore.

He had only one thing to do—to help Sora.

But...he was alone again.

Had he made a mistake letting Axel and Naminé meet? If not for that, he wouldn't be by himself now.

But Axel and Naminé were both Nobodies—beings that DiZ had said were never supposed to exist. Was that true? Was it really so wrong for Nobodies to exist?

What he'd learned from DiZ wasn't enough to go on. He'd needed to know more than DiZ—to know more about the organization. So he'd tried approaching Axel with a deal.

He'd needed information about the things DiZ knew, the things Axel knew...and the secrets of the worlds.

The deal had been a success, and they had pooled their knowledge. Thanks to that, he had been able to learn more about the truth, and more about the organization, than DiZ.

Axel had offered them information about the organization's leader, too.

Riku sat down on the boulder where Axel had been perched moments before and gazed out to where the sky met the sea.

He wanted to go back to *their* sea…their island. He wanted to run down the shore with Sora. That was the wish in his heart.

But doubt still lingered in Riku's heart, too. Had he done the right thing?

There had been no other way to awaken Sora. The only option was to destroy Roxas—or rather, to return him to Sora.

But thanks to what Axel and Naminé had said, he didn't know whether his choice was correct.

He even wondered if there had been an alternative after all.

Riku pulled his hood up. He had to be on his way quickly.

Suddenly, a high voice addressed him. "Huh, so this is where you were."

He turned. "Mickey—er, Your Majesty…"

Standing there was a dear friend of his—Mickey Mouse, the king of his own world. Still wearing the same black cloak as when they'd left Castle Oblivion, he appeared exactly the same as when Riku had last seen him, in every respect.

"You left me with your stuff and took off. Gosh, I've been lookin' all over for ya," King Mickey told him kindly. In fact, he was smiling. "Gonna give a fella a hug this time? And no need to call me 'Your Majesty,' remember? Just Mickey."

Right…, Riku remembered. *Back in Castle Oblivion, I was so glad to see him, so glad that I wasn't alone…and I hugged him.*

But I can't do that now. And—I can't just call him "Mickey" now, either. Not when I look like this.

"Your Majesty… I…" Riku tugged his hood deeper over his face.

"Gosh, Riku, I think you gotta tell me what happened."

Riku nodded faintly.

The trio climbed up the stairs in the tower, defeating Heartless as they went.

"Take that!" Sora landed a blow with the Keyblade.

"Sora! They won't let up!" Goofy exclaimed, fending off an attack.

"Heartless, Heartless, and more Heartless! Things haven't changed one bit!" Donald complained, waving his wand about.

It was true. They'd closed that great door, and yet the worlds were still overrun with Heartless.

"Gawrsh, it's a good thing we're on the job, then." Goofy knocked another back with his shield.

"So…the worlds aren't at peace after all?" Sora said mostly to himself.

His companions exchanged a troubled glance.

"Master Yen Sid oughta be able to tell us what's goin' on."

Sora and Donald nodded. "Well, let's get to the top of this tower first!" Sora declared, heading onward and upward at a run, with the other two hot on his heels.

At last, they arrived at what seemed to be the tower's summit. Beyond the door was a small room.

"Whew…" Catching their breath after the fight up the stairs, the trio looked up—and met the level gaze of an old man with a snowy white beard and a blue robe. He reminded Sora a little bit of Merlin back in Traverse Town, but this sorcerer wore a much more severe expression, which made him terribly intimidating.

"An honor to meet you again, Master Yen Sid," Donald said, and he dropped to one knee. Goofy did the same.

"Hey there!" Sora made no such effort in his greeting. Donald grabbed at his head and forced him down to one knee, too. "What?!"

"Sora! Show some respect!" Donald hissed at him as he struggled.

"So, you are Sora?" Yen Sid asked.

Sora shook off Donald and stood up with a grin. "Pleasure to meet you, Master Yen Sid!"

Yen Sid smiled very faintly in return. "Now, then—have you seen the king?"

Goofy got to his feet and stood rigidly at attention. "We have, master, but we didn't get to talk to him."

"Yes... He's been quite busy of late." Yen Sid nodded and gestured to Donald, who was still kneeling, that his deference was enough. The sorcerer went on with a grave expression. "It would seem that the task of instructing you three falls upon my shoulders. You have a perilous journey ahead of you, and you must be well prepared."

The trio shared a glance.

"You mean...we have to go on another quest?" Sora said, dismayed. "I was hoping I'd get to find my friend Riku, so we could go back to the islands..."

"Yes, I know. But everything in your journey, Sora, is connected. Whether you will find your way back to the islands, whether you will be alone or with your friend...and whether your islands will still be as you left them..." As Yen Sid spoke, Sora kept his attention fixed on him. "The key that connects them all is you, Sora."

"I'm...the key?" Sora repeated.

"Chosen wielder of the Keyblade. You are the key that will open the door to light."

Goofy cocked his head. "But...didn't we *close* the door?"

"It doesn't make any sense that the Heartless are still around!" Donald fumed.

Yen Sid dropped his gaze momentarily and then spoke again. "Your endeavors did prevent an immense effusion of Heartless from the great darkness. Make no mistake."

That seemed reasonable. They'd defeated Ansem, after all, and closed the door.

"However, the Heartless are embodiments of darkness—and darkness lingers in every heart." Yen Sid's voice was low and ominous. "The Heartless are fewer than before, but while darkness yet exists, it will be difficult to eliminate them."

"Then that must mean...if everybody's heart was full of light, the Heartless'd go away!" Goofy said.

Yen Sid dipped his head and continued, "As ever, the Heartless roam about in search of hearts, and you must keep vigilant."

"We've got that covered, Master Yen Sid!" Goofy replied.

"However...you will have other enemies to contend with as well."

Startled, the three exchanged glances again.

"At times, if someone possessed of a strong heart and will—be they good or evil—should become a Heartless, the empty shell left behind begins to act with a will of its own. That is a Nobody."

"A Nobody?" Donald echoed.

"An empty vessel whose heart has been stolen away—a spirit whose existence lingers even as the body fades... No, in fact, Nobodies do not truly exist at all. They may seem to have feelings, but this is a ruse—they only pretend to have hearts. You must not be deceived."

Nobodies... Those who did not truly exist. They'd never heard of this before.

They couldn't have—and yet Sora felt like he knew about Nobodies from somewhere. His heart skipped a beat.

Why would hearing about these Nobodies do that to me?

"You may meet alarming numbers of common Nobodies, but they are only empty shells. They will attempt to do you harm, but before long they will dissolve into the darkness." Yen Sid paused and pointed to the empty space beside them. The hazy shape of a man in a black cloak materialized there.

"...Who's that?" Sora asked quietly. He felt as if he'd seen that figure before—but he couldn't remember.

"That is one of the powerful Nobodies who have formed a group called Organization XIII. They command the lesser Nobodies."

"Organization XIII...," Sora murmured, trying to etch the words into his mind.

"While Heartless act on instinct, Nobodies function at a higher level," Yen Sid explained. "They can think and plan. And it seems that under the instruction of Organization XIII, they are working toward a higher goal."

"Gawrsh, do we know what that might be?" Goofy asked.

Yen Sid shook his head. "We cannot begin to guess. The king sensed the danger and journeyed forth to confront it. Now he's traveling from world to world, fighting the Heartless as he searches for what Organization XIII and the Nobodies are planning."

A cabal with an unknown objective: *Organization XIII.* Sora had to wonder why his heart pounded at hearing the term.

Still, it doesn't change what our goals are, he thought. *Finding Riku and the king.*

If they found the king, who was investigating the organization, then they would learn where Riku was, too, and what the organization was planning.

"Then we'd better track down the king first!" Sora blurted with determination. Donald and Goofy looked at each other.

There was nothing to be afraid of. This wasn't a new quest. They were still on their original journey.

This was still Sora's quest to find Riku, keep his promise to Kairi, and go back to the Destiny Islands.

Jiminy Cricket hopped out then from his hiding place in Sora's pocket.

Sora was startled. "Whoa!"

"And we mustn't forget to thank Naminé." With that, Jiminy ducked back into the pocket.

"Yup, he's right," Goofy remarked. "We gotta thank Naminé."

The trio grinned at one another. Satisfied to see their optimism, Yen Sid inclined his head and indicated a door in the corner.

"Before you go, you'll need more suitable traveling clothes," he told Sora. "Those seem a bit small for you."

Donald and Goofy shared a laugh.

"It's true, Master Yen Sid," Goofy said, unable to keep a funny story to himself. "Sora's clothes ripped just now."

"I've summoned three good fairies to take care of that. They may be rather fussy about clothing, but you need only to ask and they'll create some new garments for you," Yen Sid said to Sora with care.

* * *

The pair traipsed through the heavy mist. How long would they have to make their way without even a path to follow?

"...Axel?" Naminé called out to the red-haired man striding briskly ahead of her.

He halted, but didn't turn. "What? Need a break?"

"No, that's not it..." Naminé paused, watching his broad back.

"Having second thoughts about coming with me, then?"

"...I don't regret anything," she told him, and started walking again. "Where are we going?"

"I wonder." Axel's steps resumed, too.

She wasn't sure how far they should keep going in this mist.

"What are we going to do?" Naminé pressed.

"Haven't decided yet." Axel's pace remained steady this time.

"Roxas won't be coming back."

At that, Axel stopped in his tracks and looked back at her. "That was his—DiZ's plan, wasn't it? I remember that much."

His expression was hard, closed like a fortress. Seeing that, it was impossible to believe that Axel had no heart.

Heart. She rolled the word around in her mind. What did that mean, anyway? What was a heart?

"Riku's all alone now."

"That's what's bothering you?" Axel laughed softly, watching her downturned face. "He's human, you know. Not a Nobody."

"But still..." Naminé trailed off.

Axel hounded her further. "Even if he looks like that now."

"How he looks has nothing to do with it."

Naminé was certain of that. *So long as he still has his heart, his appearance doesn't matter*, she repeated to herself.

And then, realizing something, she raised her head. "Hey, Axel. If we had hearts—"

"Well, we don't. Got it memorized?" Axel interrupted bluntly.

"And you know, traitors to the organization—for the record. Do you know what that means?"

"Yes, I know."

"Then keep walking."

Naminé bit her lip and plodded onward.

When Sora, Donald, and Goofy entered the back room, three fairies who gave the impression of sweet old aunties greeted them with bright smiles. In their colored robes and hats—one green, one blue, and one red—they immediately began chattering.

"Why, look who's here—Sora, Donald, and Goofy." The first to speak was the one in red.

"If you're looking for new clothes, you've come to the right place!" said the one in blue.

"I'll take care of the designing!" the one in green gushed.

"Wait, wait, slow down!" Sora said, a bit flustered. "Can you tell me your names?"

The fairies introduced themselves self-importantly.

"I'm Merryweather."

"I'm Flora."

"And I'm Fauna."

They seemed to be rather flighty fairies. So the one in the blue was Merryweather, the red was Flora, and the green was Fauna.

"Well, Sora, why don't we get started?" Fauna waved her slender magic wand, and Sora's entire outfit turned green.

"Oh, that will never do!" This time Merryweather's wand turned Sora's garments blue.

"You two haven't the foggiest idea what you're doing," Flora declared, and with a flick of her wrist, Sora's clothes turned red.

"No, this is much better!"

"Is it?"

"Oh, what is that?"

"This'll do it!"

The barrage of magic continued, and Sora's clothes shifted through colors so fast his eyes hurt. "Aw, c'mon, would you just decide?" he complained.

"Very well… All together now, dears. No more squabbling!" Flora said, and the other two bobbed their heads in agreement. "Here goes!"

The three magic wands shot out jets of sparkles, and Sora's outfit settled into a stylish black, with trimming here and there in different colors.

"Oh my!"

"Not bad at all."

"Oh yes, he does look dashing."

In response, Sora struck a smart pose, showing off the new threads. His two friends cracked up.

"Hey! Don't laugh at me!"

"But…!" Donald couldn't contain his quacking laughter.

"Looks pretty good, doesn't it?"

"Yup," Goofy agreed.

The fairies seemed satisfied, too.

Sora examined his new clothes and hopped to test the fit.

Outside the window, a suspicious shape watched the scene. But those inside never noticed.

"Oh, and Master Yen Sid's got something for you, too," Fauna said, excited.

"Wow! Thanks, Flora, Fauna, Merryweather!" Sora exclaimed.

"You're very welcome."

The three fairies happily waved to him, the sleeves of their robes fluttering. Sora bowed to them like a prince at a great ball and rushed back out to the sorcerer's room.

The men in black cloaks gathered in the hall of spotless white marble. Their hoods hid their faces—and their expressions. Only six of the thirteen seats were occupied. The five lost at Castle Oblivion; number 13, Roxas; and number 8, Axel, were gone.

Number 2, Xigbar, opened the discussion. "So the Keyblade's on the move."

"Isn't that part of the plan?" Xaldin said, number 3.

"Losing number thirteen—well, Roxas—sure wasn't," Xigbar shot back, then turned his gaze downward. "We should have made sure our little hero stayed incomplete."

"What about Axel?" Number 9, Demyx, softly mentioned the last missing member.

Luxord, number 10, answered bluntly from his low-ranking seat, "He's apparently betrayed us."

"...Betrayed us, hmm?" rumbled number 1—Xemnas.

"Really? Him?" Demyx practically squealed.

"He was involved in the incident at Castle Oblivion... I warned you he had a hand in the demise of Marluxia and the others, and yet someone failed to eliminate him." Saïx, number 7, glared at Xigbar from under his hood with a sharp glint in his eyes.

"Hey, he's the only one who's had direct contact with the Keyblade wielder," Xigbar replied, unruffled.

"Observe them." Xemnas issued the order quietly.

"Saïx, you go after Axel. Demyx, you follow the kid." Xigbar translated it for the rest of them as if he were privy to Xemnas's thoughts.

"The kid? Roxas, you mean?" Demyx got to his feet.

"Yes... That's right. Roxas." Xigbar smiled darkly and exchanged a glance with Xemnas.

"So what do you think, Master Yen Sid?" Sora, freshly outfitted, ran up to the sorcerer.

"Oh, quite good indeed," Yen Sid replied, moving to the window. "Here—this is my final gift before you depart."

Floating outside the wide-open casement was the Gummi Ship.

Donald squawked in delight and dashed to the window.

"All right! Let's get going!" Sora seemed ready to jump straight out the window as he waited for confirmation from Donald and Goofy.

"Now, now, hold on a moment," Yen Sid said reprovingly. "Thanks to your previous endeavors, the worlds have returned to their original states—which means the pathways between them have disappeared."

Was he saying that they couldn't simply travel from world to world like before? Sora's shoulders slumped.

"That's a problem...," Donald remarked, leaning out the window to stare at the ship.

"Have no fear. If what the king suspected proves true, the worlds will have prepared new pathways, which you should be able to use by unlocking certain gates. As for how to unlock them, the Keyblade will serve as your guide."

The weapon in Sora's hand gleamed.

"Though the worlds may seem far apart and out of reach," Yen Sid said, "they all remain bound by invisible ties—as do our hearts."

Sora nodded. "Our hearts...are connected."

He was linked to Riku...and to Kairi and to King Mickey. And to all the people they'd met on their journey...

"Precisely," Yen Sid said. "But be warned—the Heartless and the Nobodies will be using their own paths, Corridors of Darkness, to move from world to world. And they may be trying to link their corridors to the gates between the worlds."

Sora nodded again, more forcefully this time.

"Now, that is all I can tell you. Go forth, Sora, Donald, Goofy. Your friends and the worlds are waiting."

The trio looked at one another and nodded in unison.

"Okay, we're off!" Sora declared, and leaped out to the Gummi Ship as it floated up to meet them.

Donald and Goofy briskly saluted Yen Sid, who smiled at them in return, then jumped out after Sora.

The humming of the engine grew steadily louder, and the Gummi Ship took off into the Ocean Between.

Just then, an ink-black shadow fluttered to the floor in the middle of the fairies' room.

"Goodness—what is that?" Merryweather edged back from it in apprehension.

A solitary raven clutched a length of black cloth in its claws and cawed a sinister *kraak*.

The fairies eyed the cloth fearfully. "Haven't we seen that somewhere before...?" Merryweather said.

"I believe so...," Fauna mused. "I wonder whose..."

"Is it Mal—?"

As Merryweather began to utter a name, Flora rushed to interrupt. "No! We mustn't remember her name! Oh, I've got a terrible feeling about this!" Shivering, she crossed her arms and hugged herself.

"Ooh, she was a mean ol' witch. Oh no, the memories are coming back! This is no good! What'll we do?" Merryweather fretted, beginning to pace.

Between them, the black cloth slowly squirmed...into the form of a person.

"We've got to tell Master Yen Sid!" cried Fauna.

"Yes—that's what we'll do!" Flora agreed. The two of them flew out of the room, leaving behind the black cloth—and Merryweather.

The cloth, which had taken the shape of a dress, lifted into the air by itself and transformed into a certain witch who should have stayed lost in their memories.

Merryweather screamed the name of the enchantress who had imprisoned their beloved princess within tangles of cursed thorns.

The princess was called Aurora, and the witch was called—

"Maleficent!"

Merryweather scurried out after the others, leaving Maleficent to survey the room with some degree of familiarity.

And then she let out a high, cruel laugh.

HOLLOW BASTION

RIKU AND KING MICKEY EACH SAT ON A BOULDER, watching the sunset.

...Just like Riku used to do with Sora and Kairi.

How long ago was that now? It must have been ages, and yet the memory felt like it had happened just yesterday.

I'd like to go home, if we can, Riku thought. *But the way I am now, I can't.*

This was the path he'd chosen for himself.

"We'd better get going," King Mickey said to Riku.

"Right." Riku got to his feet.

They'd spoken about many things—about everything that had happened and what might lie ahead.

In truth, he wanted to go with King Mickey, but there were things that he had to take care of on his own.

"If you take the Corridors of Darkness, you can come and go between the worlds wherever you want. You know how to do that, right?"

"Yeah."

Once, being around King Mickey had been painful enough for Riku to travel those corridors alone. And now, because of that, he'd gained enormous power—and the form of a different person.

He wasn't sure if that was good or bad.

Only a sliver of sun remained above the horizon, and dusk painted the sky pale violet.

"Your Majesty, I want you to promise me something."

At that, King Mickey finally stood up. "What's that?"

"Even...even if you meet Sora or the others, promise you won't tell them about me?"

"Okay. I won't." King Mickey gave him a solemn nod.

Riku began to walk away across the sand. "Well, I'm off."

"Riku!" he heard King Mickey call after him. "We'll be apart, y'know...but it'll be all right."

Riku looked back at him.

"You're not alone, Riku."

He'd heard those words before.

That was what the king had told him in that castle—Castle Oblivion.

"Yeah. I know. You and Sora and everyone else...you're always with me." Riku smiled.

King Mickey nodded in reply.

"See you, Your Majesty." With that, Riku stepped into the gap in space yawning before him—the Corridor of Darkness.

The Gummi Ship sailed on through the Ocean Between.

"Can't see a thing!" Donald announced with his bill against the porthole.

Sora joined him and smushed his face against the glass to look outside. "Nope, nothing. But King Mickey got the Gummi Ship all ready for us, didn't he?"

"Sora, Donald! C'mere! I can see something thataway!" Goofy called, likewise pressed against the opposite porthole.

"Where?"

"What? Where?"

The other two dashed over to him. Donald climbed atop Goofy, and Sora poked his head up under Goofy's snout.

"You're squishin' me!" Goofy protested.

"You're in the way!" snapped Donald.

"Look, there it is!"

All pressed up against the little porthole, pushing and shoving, they could see a world floating in the distance.

"Only one?" Sora complained as the Gummi Ship drifted closer.

"That's not enough," Donald said glumly, and finally hopped down off Goofy.

Goofy gazed fixedly at the lone world. "But...I think it's a world we know."

"I dunno..." Sora sounded a bit uncertain, his nose still on the window.

"Look, there's a castle in the middle of it," Goofy pointed out.

Donald promptly clambered atop him again and squinted. "It's Hollow Bastion!" he exclaimed, bouncing.

"You're right!" After Sora's head knocked into Goofy's chin, he happily thought aloud, "I wonder how everyone's doing..."

The Gummi Ship sped closer to Hollow Bastion.

"Maleficent! Maleficent?!" A harsh male voice echoed through the quiet halls.

This was a place where evil had once dwelled, the empty fortress—Hollow Bastion.

Pete glanced furtively about the grand hall, wandering around at a loss.

The castle was much changed from when Sora had come in search of Kairi. No one seemed to be here at all, leaving it even more lonely and decrepit.

"Maybe they really did finish her off?" Pete muttered nervously. "And this castle sure ain't like I heard about neither. No shine, no nothin'... Now what's gonna happen to our plan...?"

Crestfallen, he hung his head.

An enormous window in the grand hall overlooked the town. Steam rose from the buildings below, proving that people lived there. The streets even looked cheerful—which also didn't match up with what Maleficent had told him.

A single raven alighted on the window ledge and made a raucous caw.

"...Maleficent?" Pete mumbled, and the bird flew into the hall.

Sora bounded out of the Gummi Ship and hopped again for sheer joy. "It *is* Hollow Bastion!"

Donald and Goofy followed him out and took in the scene.

"Gawrsh, it looks kinda different now," Goofy wondered aloud, gazing up at the castle in the distance.

"I hope Leon and the gang are doing okay." Hoping to find them right away, Donald took off over the brick-paved square—and leaped back in surprise. *"Quack!"*

"What's the matter, Donald?" Then Sora jumped, too. "Whoa!"

There was a mass of Heartless in front of them.

"Guess we better gear up for more fightin', huh?" Goofy said under his breath.

"All right—here we go!" Sora called. They charged, Donald with his wand and Goofy with his shield, and before long the swarm was defeated, releasing the trapped hearts and dissipating.

"That was quick!" Sora grinned, resting the Keyblade across his shoulders.

"I guess this is the town market," Donald said, looking around. Heartless didn't often come where there were lots of people—the same as Traverse Town.

"Unca Donald!" someone called suddenly.

Donald turned. *"Wak?"*

The voice belonged to one of his nephews, Louie, perched on a shop counter.

"Gee, it's been a long time!" Goofy ran up to the window.

Sora followed. "So you're still running a store, huh?"

"Yep. Good to see you, Sora!"

Apparently the brothers Huey, Dewey, and Louie managed shops here and there around town.

"Unca Scrooge is here, too!" Dewey called from across the street.

"He is?!" Donald whirled.

"Who's that?" Sora whispered to Goofy. The name wasn't familiar.

"Donald's uncle. He's a big businessman!" Goofy replied. "Before the Heartless showed up, he was travelin' on the Gummi Ship with the king. He was gonna help set up a traffic system."

"Transit system!" Donald corrected him peevishly.

"Unca Scrooge's right over thataway!" Huey pointed, and Donald scurried off.

Sora and Goofy rushed to catch up. "Slow down, Donald!"

"Uncle Scrooge?" Donald called to a gentleman duck in a silk hat in front of a building that appeared to be an enormous freezer.

"What's all the racket?" The gentleman in question turned around. He had some kind of ice pop in his hand. "Why, if it isn't Donald. Hello there, lad!"

Scrooge hopped in surprise, just like Donald often did, and smiled warmly. The family resemblance was striking. He wore a pair of spectacles and a blue suit.

"And Goofy, too. Aye, you both look hale and hearty!"

"So do you, Uncle Scrooge."

But Scrooge's face fell at Donald's reply. "Ah, if only I was… I've been trying to re-create my favorite old-time ice cream. Thought I'd make a pretty penny…"

"Ice cream?!" Sora blurted, poking his head in between Donald and Goofy.

"Who's this now?" Scrooge asked.

"I'm Sora!" After this brief introduction, he stared intently at the ice pop Scrooge was holding.

"He's our friend," Donald explained.

Scrooge peered with interest at Sora. "Do you like ice cream, lad?"

"Yeah!" Sora nodded, his gaze intensifying. It had been forever since he'd had a treat like that, he thought, unconsciously leaning in.

And yet he got the feeling he had had one somewhere… It must have been home on Destiny Islands, and yet it wasn't…

"What's wrong, Sora?" asked Goofy, seeing Sora's confusion.

"Oh—it's nothing. Um, Mr. Scrooge, could I have one?" Sora's expression returned to a hopeful grin.

Scrooge heaved a sigh. "Well, you can have this one, but…you see…"

"Really? Thanks, Mr. Scrooge!" Sora took it from Scrooge's hand.

"Oh no, I should warn you—"

"I can't wait!" Ignoring Scrooge's attempts to stop him, Sora chomped down on the ice cream bar. "......Ugh!"

He held it at arm's length and scrunched up his face in disgust.

Donald took the ice pop and sniffed it before taking a bite. "...It's awful!" He made the same face as Sora, and then Goofy tried it.

"Gee, that's pretty bad...," Goofy said mournfully.

"What *is* that?! It doesn't taste like ice cream! It's bitter!" Sora complained.

"I did try to warn you...," Scrooge said with another sigh, and his shoulders slumped. "I haven't been able to get it right."

"What kind of ice cream is it supposed to be?" Donald asked.

"I don't quite remember, myself."

"...That would make it pretty tough." Goofy crossed his arms and sighed, too.

Beside him, Sora stamped his foot. "Aww, I want ice cream!" he yelled at the sky.

"Well, do ye mind waiting a bit?" Scrooge said. "I think I can—no, I'm *sure* I can—re-create that flavor properly!"

Goofy nodded. "Guess we gotta wait."

"See you later, Uncle Scrooge," Donald said.

"Aye..." Scrooge nodded weakly, and the trio started heading farther into town.

"I want ice cream! C'mon! Ice cream!" Sora kept insisting, his sweet tooth getting the better of him.

Goofy cocked his head. "You really like ice cream that much?"

"Everyone likes ice cream!"

"*Wak!* Ain't that the truth!" Donald agreed.

"See? It's sweet and cold and...huh?" Sora paused, confusion creeping over his face again.

"What? That's ice cream, all right."

"Hmm... Yeah, sweet and cold and...I dunno." It felt like he was forgetting something. *Cold, sweet, and...what else?* "Oh well. That's what makes ice cream great!"

He nodded decisively to himself. Just then…

"Sora!"

The voice came from above. They found the source on the rooftops—a girl with short black hair.

"Yuffie?!"

"Hey there!" She hopped down lightly and sprinted over.

"Looks like you're doing okay," Sora said.

"What'd you expect?" Yuffie grinned.

"How are Leon and everyone?" asked Donald, waddling up to meet her.

"Just great! Hey, Sora, did you get a little taller?" Yuffie stood next to Sora, comparing their heights.

"Heh-heh-heh," Sora laughed boastfully, but then asked her a serious question. "Hey, Yuffie, have you seen Riku or King Mickey?"

"Nope." She shook her head.

So…they probably hadn't been here. Sora slumped in disappointment. "Oh."

Yuffie smiled at him. "I had a feeling I'd see you guys again, though."

"We may never meet again, but we'll never forget each other," Sora said, deepening his voice and affecting a serious manner. "Right?"

That was what Leon had told him when they said good-bye at Hollow Bastion before.

"Is that your Leon impression?"

"Yep! You got it!"

Sora and Yuffie shared a glance and giggled.

"Everybody's over at Merlin's house. C'mon!" Yuffie took off, and Sora, Donald, and Goofy tagged along behind her.

In a room made of white marble, a large mirror reflected Demyx as he prepared to leave for the mission. He took particular care with his hairstyle, painstakingly manipulating the brown strands with a comb to make them stand straight up. Saïx observed him from behind with what appeared to be distaste. In stark contrast to Demyx, Saïx left his long blue hair unstyled. The X-shaped scar on his forehead was all the style he needed.

"What d'you want? I'm kinda busy." Irritated, Demyx turned around.

Instead of responding, the other man simply disappeared.

"Excuse me?!" Demyx shouted at the space where Saïx had been standing.

And then, as if to take Saïx's place, Xigbar appeared with his hood low over his eyes. "Ready yet?"

"...Yeah, yeah, just about," Demyx replied apathetically. "Y'know, Xigbar, I don't really think I'm the best suited for tailing somebody..."

"Orders are orders, and you can't go against the big man himself. Or did you forget?"

"...Hmph."

Not the most satisfying answer. Demyx scowled and leaned on the sitar in his hand.

"Anyway, you're going to be saying hello first," Xigbar added.

"Huh?"

"The hero and his little entourage are out and about. Saïx heard their voices."

"Uh-huh...," Demyx said, more like a sigh than a response, and frowned.

He couldn't hear the voices.

He may have been assigned a number, but he knew perfectly well that he just wasn't cut out for fighting. All he could do was control water by playing music. He didn't think of himself as especially strong. And shadowing the Keyblade wielder—or rather, Roxas—really didn't sound like much fun.

Still, he couldn't defy the organization. For that sole reason, he had to follow his orders.

"Time to get going," Xigbar said.

"Okay, okay..." Demyx shouldered his sitar and vanished.

"He really is a handful." Xigbar chuckled to himself and likewise disappeared from the room.

Inside the little house, Leon, Aerith, and Cid were all somberly studying a big computer screen.

Aerith let out a tiny sigh, and the next moment, the door banged open.

The three inside started, ready to defend themselves, but it was only Yuffie, standing there with a grin.

"Don't scare people like that, Yuffie...," Leon scolded. Then three more people crowded in behind her—Sora, Donald, and Goofy.

"Meet the Hollow Bastion Restoration Committee!" the ninja announced to the newcomers.

"Oh! We've missed you." Aerith greeted them with a cheerful smile.

"Well, looks like you're all in shipshape condition," Cid announced, getting up from his chair in front of the screen.

"You could say hi, too, Leon," Yuffie prompted.

Leon folded his arms sternly and muttered, "I knew it."

"Knew what?" asked Sora, clueless.

"Just recently, everyone suddenly remembered you three, all at the same time."

The three in question shared a puzzled look.

"You...remembered?" Sora said. "Hey, does that mean you *forgot* about us?"

Donald hopped with anger. "Gee, thanks!"

"We're sorry." Aerith bowed her head contritely.

But...how had anyone forgotten them in the first place?

"So where've you guys been all this time?" Yuffie asked them.

"We were sleepin', I guess," Goofy said, sounding fairly unconcerned.

"Not a care in the world for you guys, huh?" Cid remarked.

"It's all right now." Aerith smiled sweetly at them. "We're all together again, aren't we?"

"Yeah. We're glad to see you guys, too!" Sora agreed.

Seeing everyone gathered here lifted his spirits. He'd been afraid they would never see one another again.

"Oh yeah— Um, we're looking for Riku and King Mickey. Have you seen 'em?"

Aerith and the others silently checked to see if anyone had, then shook their heads.

"Oh, okay…" Sora's head drooped in disappointment.

"Let us know if there's anything we can do to help, okay?" Aerith said, stepping toward him.

"Yeah. Thanks."

I'm glad she wants to help, Sora thought.

"Don't go thankin' us just yet…," Cid cautioned with a pointed glance Leon's way, plunking down in his chair again.

"This town has a problem. A big problem," Leon explained for him.

"You mean, like Nobodies? And Heartless?" Sora guessed.

"Right! Exactly!" Yuffie leaned in.

"Sounds like a job for us."

"Then let's cut to the chase," Leon said. "Sora, Donald, Goofy—we were hoping you might give us a hand around here."

Sora crossed his arms and smirked at how earnestly Leon posed the question. "Like we're gonna say no?"

"Hmm… I forgot who we're dealing with." Leon moved toward the door. "Come with me to the bailey—there's something you need to see."

Just as Sora and his friends went to follow him, there was a mysterious *poof!* and a cloud of white smoke blocked their way.

"Oh-ho, so there you are."

Standing in front of them was Merlin the magician.

"Merlin!" Donald ran up to him. The wizard was his own teacher and a great magician.

"Sora and the gang said they're gonna help out!" Yuffie excitedly informed him.

"Oh, splendid. We're counting on you."

"Yes, sir!" the trio chorused.

"Ah, Aerith—did you give them those little things?"

"Oh!" At Merlin's reminder, Aerith reached into her pocket for something.

"Here… They're presents for you." She held out three cards. "Leon thought you might like to have them."

Sora, Donald, and Goofy each took one. Sora's card had his name on it with a picture of the castle and a few words… "Hollow Bastion Restoration Committee Honorary Member!" he read proudly.

"Membership cards!" Donald crowed, holding his up over his head.

Goofy excitedly clutched his in both hands. "Pretty neat, huh?"

"Thanks, Le… Huh? Did he leave without us?!" Sora fretted, finding that Leon was no longer in the house. The man hadn't even waited to see if they were with him. "Uh-oh!"

The trio ran outside—but the street was swarming with Heartless.

"*Wak!*" Donald jumped at the sheer numbers.

"Gee, why are there still so many Heartless around?" Goofy complained, slumping at the thought of yet another skirmish. It seemed like there were only more of them since they'd closed the gate.

"Well, we'd better find Leon!" Sora said, brandishing his Keyblade. The other two nodded.

From Merlin's house, the bailey was down a few alleys and up some stairs.

"C'mon! Let's go!" Heartless fell left and right as they made their way toward it.

He ran up the steps to the top of a massive wall. From there, in the distance, he could see a huge castle—one he recognized.

"That's where we fought Maleficent, isn't it?" Sora said, not taking his eyes off it.

Goofy leaned out a bit. "Is this the castle wall?"

"Yeah, 'cos we're going to the bailey!" Donald told him with an all-knowing air.

Their fight against Maleficent seemed so long ago.

As Sora gazed pensively at the castle, Goofy called from behind, "Leon must be waitin' for us. Let's go."

"Right!"

They continued until they could see part of the stronghold in front of them.

"Is that the bailey?" Donald asked without slowing down.

"It's gotta be," Goofy replied.

"That took you long enough."

They found Leon staring at the castle from the stronghold, just like they'd been doing.

"Look at that." Leon pointed to a writhing mass filling the grounds around the castle. "We want to restore Hollow Bastion to what it used to be. Or who knows—maybe something even better. There's still a lot to do, but we can handle everything...except for *that*."

He shook his head at the horde of silver creatures below.

"Are those all...Nobodies?" Sora murmured.

Leon nodded.

Those creatures they'd fought in Twilight Town—not Heartless, but Nobodies, as Yen Sid had called them.

"*Wak!* But it's full of Heartless, too!" Donald had spied the swarm and sprang up.

So for some reason Hollow Bastion was teeming with both Nobodies *and* Heartless.

"Sora, do you know what's going on?" asked Leon.

"This guy called Pete is up to something with the Heartless as part of his plan. But he's pretty dumb. I think we can deal with him. What we need to worry about is..." Sora folded his arms and inclined his head.

Goofy finished the sentence for him. "Those Nobodies and the Organization XIII fellas in charge of 'em..." He sighed, and then—

"You rang?" An unfamiliar voice addressed them in a deep, intimidating baritone.

"You're doing well." The next greeting belonged to a different man.

"Who's there?!" Sora shouted.

"It's a reunion. We should celebrate." The deep voice gave a quiet, sinister chuckle.

"Sora!" Leon called.

He turned to find a cluster of Nobodies.

"*Wa-waaak!*" Donald jumped in alarm, clutching his wand tightly.

"I'll take care of this side!" Gunblade in hand, Leon rushed at the Nobodies.

Sora charged in the other direction. "Okay—I've got this side!"

"*Fire!*"

The Nobody slid right under Donald's spell. Their movements were so strange they were almost impossible to hit.

"Quit wriggling around!" Sora yelled as he caught one with the Keyblade.

"The Keyblade—a marvelous weapon...," said that voice.

"Show yourselves!" Sora demanded, still relentlessly bashing Nobodies.

"Heh-heh..."

The mocking laughter seemed to echo from inside his own skull. The boy shook his head.

That voice...that laugh. It was horribly unsettling.

And not just unsettling—something else...

"Sora!"

Leon called him back to the present. When Sora turned, he saw...a pack of men in black cloaks.

They were standing on the opposite wall, looking down at Sora and his friends.

"Organization XIII!" cried Goofy.

There were six of them, hoods obscuring their faces.

"Oh, good—I can take you all out at once!" Sora shouted, losing himself in his frustration.

He couldn't stand the sound of their laughter.

"What a shame... And here I thought we could be friends," the man in the center said, chuckling again as a dark space yawned behind them. The figures disappeared into it.

"Hey, wait!" Donald shouted, dashing ahead to pursue them.

"Careful, there." One of the organization materialized again right in front of Donald's bill.

"Donald!" Behind him, Sora stood with the Keyblade ready. "You—move!"

"That's not very nice, shutting me down like that," the man teased.

"I mean it! Get out of the way!"

"You can talk all you want, but you can't actually do anything about it, so..." The man shrugged as if Sora's threat was of no concern whatsoever.

"Then we'll *make* you move!" snapped Donald. *"Fire!"*

He waved his wand, but the spurt of magic fizzled out just before reaching the man's cloak.

"Sure, that would work...if I were just any old guy. 'Cept I'm not. I'm with Organization XIII. Nothing 'any old' about me."

"Ha!" Sora barked, disgusted. "That's real tough talk from someone who stood on the sidelines watching his Nobody flunkies do all the fighting!"

"Oh no...I think you got the wrong impression," the man said, completely unruffled, and tilted his head thoughtfully. "Why don't I remind you how tough this crowd really is?"

"Remind me?" Sora echoed.

What's he mean by that? What did we forget? What have I *forgotten?*

"*Bwa-ha-ha-ha-ha!*" the man burst out laughing. "That's right—he used to give me the exact same look."

Sora glared at him. "So, you think you can psych me out by saying really random stuff?"

"Well...who knows?" he said smugly, as if to provoke Sora further, and raised one arm. Inky darkness seeped up from under his feet. "Be a good boy, now!"

The man vanished, seeming to melt away into the blackness.

"Wait!" Sora dashed to where the man had been standing, and Donald skidded after him, but the man was gone without a trace.

"That was weird… Who gave him the same look?" Sora lowered the Keyblade. *Who was he talking about?*

"I think maybe he was just tryin' to confuse ya," Goofy assured him, cocking his head.

"Yeah, you're right. There's only one me!" Sora nodded to himself and helped Donald up from where he'd fallen.

As he did, the committee membership card slipped out of his pocket.

"Oops. Don't wanna lose that…" Sora picked it up—and it began to glow. "Huh?"

Surprised, he let go of it, and the card floated into the air. At the same time, a shine enveloped the Keyblade, too.

"What's going on?" Leon ran up to them.

"I think, maybe…" Sora held the key aloft, and a beam of light shot from it. Ahead, the glow from the membership card took the shape of a keyhole. Light struck light with the click of a lock opening. "Yeah, I get it," he murmured as he lowered his hand.

"So this is one o' those gates that Master Yen Sid was talking about?" Goofy said, watching the luminous keyhole dissipate.

Sora nodded. "It's gotta be."

"Oh, boy! We did it!" Donald struck a victorious pose.

"Sorry to run, Leon… But it looks like the other worlds are calling." Sora waved to him.

"Yeah, looks that way."

"We'll be back!" Donald gestured with his wand rather than his hand.

"Organization XIII… They sound like serious trouble," Leon said. "Be careful out there."

"We will." Sora nodded forcefully. "See you soon." He looked up at the space where the keyhole had been. Maybe the king was there through the gate…and Riku, too. The thought made his heart pound.

But… Who was it?

Who had that man been talking about?

CHAPTER 3

OLYMPUS COLISEUM

THE PAIR WALKED IN SILENCE.

The stagnant air made it a little hard to breathe. There was nothing to be seen in any direction—only a thick, gloomy mist obscuring their vision.

It felt like they'd been walking in circles for ages. Naminé tried to look around. Maybe they really had, she thought.

"Axel?"

"...Yeah?" His steps never paused.

"Where are you going?"

"...Our base of operations," Axel replied, over his shoulder this time. "What are you going to do?"

She gazed straight at him. "What do you mean?"

"If I return with you in tow, I get to live without being branded as a traitor," he said with a wry grin.

"Maybe. Axel, what do you want to do?"

"Avoid being eliminated ideally."

"So you're offering me up to the organization?"

"...Well, you see any other options?" His expression was frozen in a forced smile.

He had no ideas. He didn't know what to do.

And he had no heart and thus no emotions to guide him, either.

"I have a request," Naminé said, determined. "I want...to meet Kairi."

Axel frowned. Naminé was a Nobody. If she met Kairi, her true self...Naminé would disappear. "Are you serious?"

"Well..." She looked at the ground. "Isn't that only natural?"

"Then what did you wanna come with me for?" Axel flung his arms out angrily.

"Because... Because you seemed lonely."

"*What?*" The irritated furrow between his brows deepened.

"You seemed lonely," Naminé repeated, raising her eyes.

"Lonely? Me, a Nobody, *lonely*? That doesn't even make sense!"

"You know, Axel... I wonder if we really do have hearts after all."

"Yeah, well... That's impossible." He turned away from her.

We don't have hearts.

Still... I know that feeling. I was lonely. I've been lonely since Roxas went away...!

Does that mean I have a heart? Is that what makes me feel this way?

"Axel...," Naminé began.

"Sorry to bother you when you're so busy, but..."

The sentence was finished not by Naminé's voice, but a man's. Axel looked up to see someone else he knew.

He hadn't even sensed him coming!

"Saïx...!" he snarled, and the other man slowly lowered his hood, smiling serenely.

Long blue hair escaped from the hood, but it didn't hide the scar on his forehead.

"Naminé, run!"

She flinched at Axel's shout and took off. Ahead of her was a portal in the air. "Axel...!"

"It's okay—go! I'll catch up."

Naminé nodded and jumped into the gateway.

"So you're trying to play the hero now, too?" Saïx said flatly, staring hard at Axel.

Number 8 gripped his chakrams, hoping he'd be able to buy some time. Enough for Naminé to find Riku, at least. He edged backward, step by tiny step.

If he was being honest, Axel didn't think he could win against Saïx. The best he could do was to find an opening and make a break for it.

"What are you going to do now?" Saïx asked, watching the portal close with no discernible reaction.

"Nothing that's any of your business."

Saïx shifted his shoulders. "I beg to differ, if you're going to betray the organization."

"...So, are you saying I'm not already a traitor?" Axel smirked.

"We can't let you turn the hero into a Heartless."

"Huh? What're you talking about?"

Apparently they weren't having the same conversation.

The organization's objective was to recover Roxas—the wielder—and have him under their control. Wasn't it? Well, to be precise, the goal was to use Roxas's Keyblade to destroy the Heartless, collect all the hearts, and regain hearts for themselves.

Then did this mean…the organization had given up on Roxas? If they had Sora, they didn't need Roxas? Was that it?

"Our goals are constantly evolving," Saïx explained dispassionately, taking a step toward his retreating target.

In response, Axel leaped back. "Oh yeah? Huh… That's news to me. So, what're your orders this time? You can tell me," he mocked, as he started to create something behind Saïx. To the naked eye it appeared to be nothing but a black dot.

He'd jumped away for a reason. He just needed a little more time and distance, and the blue-haired man wasn't the type to attack without any provocation.

"My orders are to take you down!" A heavy sword materialized in Saïx's hands, and he closed the space between them in one leap.

"…Not the brightest, are you?" Now that Saïx was in very close range, Axel sprang right over him and ran. The setup he'd planted was just ahead now—a distortion in the air steadily taking shape. He knew he had no chances of defeating number 7 in a fight, but he had every confidence in his own speed and cleverness.

"What—?!" Saïx whirled around. But Axel had already plunged into the warp.

The trio disembarked from the Gummi Ship into a world they'd never seen before.

"Gee, this place is new…" Goofy cocked his head. The almost completely lightless expanse was strewn with boulders. It seemed to be a cave.

"There's the way out!" Donald pointed to a large, shining gateway at the top of a staircase.

"Looks like there's a door over there in the rock, too," Goofy said, directing their attention in the opposite direction. Over that way, they could see a sliding door made from a single block of stone.

"Which way should we go?" wondered a confused Sora between the two.

Just then, a scream pierced the air.

"Whoa! Sora—Heartless!" Goofy raised his shield and charged. Near the stone door, a woman was on the ground, surrounded by Heartless.

"*Wa-wa-wa-waaak!*" Donald joined Goofy fending off the Heartless.

"Are you all right?" Sora went to help her up, but the woman shook her head and stood on her own.

"Thanks. But I'm fine... Who are you supposed to be?"

"I'm Sora. That's Donald, and that's Goofy. We're trying to find our friends."

She nodded and glanced up to the door atop the stairs before introducing herself. "Name's Megara, but you can call me Meg. I'm a friend of our local hero."

"Hero?" Donald regarded her curiously.

"Yeah. The hero of this world... But he's about to run out of heroics."

"Who is he?" asked Goofy.

"Hercules. He spends all day, every day, duking it out in the Coliseum up there." Still staring at the bright door, Megara sighed.

The trio exchanged glances.

"Duking it out with who?" Sora asked. "Heartless?"

"No— Hades just keeps sending him tough customers. Monsters, really..."

"Hades?"

At the unfamiliar name, they looked at one another again.

"The Lord of the Underworld," Megara explained. "I was on my way to have a chat with him just now. Maybe I can get him to give Hercules a breather. If anything happens to that kid..."

"Gawrsh, sounds like you're more than friends," Goofy said.

"Wh— No, we're not!" she retorted, a hint of color in her cheeks.

Sora folded his arms and looked up at the knight. "Well, we can't just leave someone down here when she's trying to help out a friend."

"But they're not just friends!" Goofy pointed out.

"Then we definitely can't!" Donald snapped.

"We'll go talk to Hades for you," Sora declared.

Megara's head rose. "Really? Well, I guess I'll take you up on that."

"Leave it to us!" Sora boastfully jabbed a thumb at his chest, and Donald and Goofy followed suit.

"Okay, let's go!" They nodded to one another and wrenched open the stone door.

At the same time, deep in the bowels of the Underworld, its ruler Hades had a visit from a familiar character.

"So, what're you gonna do about Hercules? He's makin' mince-meat outta every fighter you send." The guest was none other than Pete, pacing around restlessly and muttering to himself. "Pretty soon the Underworld's gonna be standing room only! Sheesh. I guess by now there's a whole lotta new warriors down here."

Hades scowled contemptuously at Pete's ranting. The Lord of the Dead was tall with a sickly blue complexion, and his hair blazed with hellish flames.

Before Hades and Pete was a pit spouting yellowish-green mist, along with a rotten stench. Pete scrunched up his face in response to the smell.

"...So, basically, I've got a full roster of fallen warriors to put back in the game," mused Hades.

"What d'you mean?" Pete demanded, crossing his arms in an attempt to seem confident.

"See this hole in the floor? It's a portal to the Underworld's deep-est, darkest dungeon." Hades peered down into it with a nasty grin. "Which means I can call up the baddest of the bad whenever I want."

"Ya don't say...," mumbled Pete, even as Hades's grin sent a shiver down his spine, and shrank back.

Hades let out a sinister chuckle, either at Pete's fear or at his own scheming, and waved his hand at the pit. A crackling bolt of light blasted from his hand down into the depths.

Pete crept back even farther from the uncanny roar that followed.

"...Ya don't say..." He cowered, covering his face against the awful reek and flash of eerie light.

At Hades's near-maniacal cackling, Pete peeked out from between his fingers and saw a man dressed in red and holding an enormous sword. A terrible wound to his face had permanently closed his right eye, and his graying hair was cut short. His left arm was tucked into his robes.

"Let's cut to the chase, Mr. Not-so-nice-guy. I've got a deal for you," Hades told him cheerfully. "Do what I say, and you're free as a bird, no strings attached."

The man shifted his attention from Hades to Pete.

"Eep..." Pete retreated a step, unnerved by the penetrating one-eyed gaze.

"It's a walk in the park, really," Hades went on, teeth still bared. "Go to the Coliseum and fight Hercules...to the death."

Unflinching, the man lifted the corners of his mouth into a hint of a smile. "This is my story. And you're not part of it."

He raised his sword squarely at Hades.

"Did you forget who you're talking to?! I am the Lord of the Dead!"

"Right... No wonder no one wants to die."

At that, Hades's flaming hair flared up red with anger. "You are fired!" he shouted, and lunged at the man.

Sora and his friends headed deeper and deeper into the dreary caverns, taking down Heartless along the way.

"A lady shouldn't be in a place like this all by her lonesome," Goofy

said, knocking aside with his shield any Heartless that jumped at him.

"No way, nohow!" Donald agreed, and with a flick of his wand another turned to mist.

"Anyway… D'you get the feeling we're not as strong as usual?" Goofy examined his shield as if it would tell him the reason.

"Aw, it's just your imagination," Sora replied breezily, and rested the Keyblade across his shoulders. "Or maybe it's just you?"

"Gawrsh, I guess so…" Goofy cocked his head, unconvinced.

"About this hero, though… Hercules? I wonder what he's like?" Sora gushed, obviously intrigued.

"Well, gee…" Goofy folded his arms, musing. "Probably tall and handsome, and really nice…"

"So, the complete opposite of Sora?" Donald jeered.

"Wha—? Hey!" Sora began chasing him.

"See? You attack your friends!" As Donald fled, he collided with something and fell back on his tail. *"Quack!"*

"Oops… Sorry about that." The person he'd run into bowed his head apologetically.

"Huh? …*Gah!*"

When the trio noticed the man's organization cloak, they readied their weapons again, and he took a step back.

"Retreat!" he shouted.

At that, some squirming Nobodies showed themselves, but they simply continued down the passage Sora had just come from, completely ignoring the three. The organization man followed his minions.

"What was that about?" Sora squinted after him.

"Wasn't that somebody from Organization XIII?" Goofy asked.

"Must've been…" But Sora was confused, too.

"Look, there's a door!" Donald announced, peering down where the man had been.

Sora and the other two stood before a huge door, much like the one at the gates to the Underworld where they'd found Megara.

"Ya think...Hades is through there?" Goofy said.

Sora and Donald nodded. They opened the door and peeked through the gap.

"Someone needs help in there!" cried Donald.

In the large round chamber, a man with graying hair was lying on the floor. Beside him stood another man, tall and bluish skinned. The trio scurried inside.

"What do you think you're doing?" The tall man had flames for hair, which blazed an angry red. Hades glared at the newcomers.

"I could ask you the same thing!" Sora retorted, and dashed in front of the man on the ground to cover him with the Keyblade.

Someone else popped out of Hades's shadow. "It's *you* pip-squeaks!"

"Pete!" cried Donald and Goofy.

"I knew you were up to no good!" Sora braced for a fight.

"Hades!" Pete yelled. "It's them! The ones tryin' to interfere with our plan!"

"Oh yeah? That so?" Arms crossed, Hades grinned viciously. "I take it you're friends of Hercules or something?"

"So, you're Hades? Well, we're here to talk to you," Sora began.

"No... Go, now...," the fallen man muttered to him.

"We can't do that!" Goofy went to help him up, but Hades glided over and tossed Goofy aside.

"Blizzard!" Donald flung out a spell, but the blast of ice melted away before it even touched Hades's robes.

"What's going on...?" Sora sprang forward to attack—or tried to. The strength drained from his legs, and instead he tumbled over.

"We can't do anything!" shouted Donald, waving his wand in vain.

"I feel kinda funny...," Sora mumbled. He couldn't even seem to get up.

"You finally noticed! See, that's the thing. In the Underworld, heroes are zeroes. Comes with the territory!" Hades crowed, and struck at Sora.

"Ngh!"

The one who blocked the attack from Hades was the man who had been on the floor.

Hades laughed, knowing he'd scarcely have to lift a finger. "Still got that much fight in ya…?"

"Run. Now!" the warrior in red shouted.

"But—," Sora protested as he finally got to his feet.

"We can't fight him here! Listen to me. We have to go!"

Sora, Donald, and Goofy gave in and fled the chamber.

"What about that guy back there?" Sora worried, checking over his shoulder—and the man in question was only a little ways behind them.

Goofy swiveled his head, too, ears flapping, and grinned at Sora. "Oh, good, he made it!"

Donald stopped to catch a gasping breath. "Did we lose him?"

"Don't count on it," the man replied.

"He's right. C'mon, the party's just getting started."

Hades had appeared beside the magician without a sound other than those mocking words.

"*Wak!*"

Pete brought up the rear with a passel of Heartless. "Hold it right there!"

"Run for it!" Sora cried. The four of them started to do just that, only to find Heartless in front of them, too. "Whoa!"

Sora skidded to a halt, but the mysterious man was already charging ahead to mow down the Heartless with one stroke of his huge sword.

"Wow!" Donald marveled.

"Let's go!" The man wasted no time, and they scrambled to follow him.

"Hey, mister, you're pretty good," Sora said as he caught up. The man cracked a lopsided smile.

"Say, are you a hero?" Goofy asked, and at that the man stopped in his tracks. The other three paused with him as if following his lead.

"I'm no hero. I'm just…Auron."

"Auron?" Donald echoed.

"That's my name." He sounded a little embarrassed.

The trio confirmed that they'd all had the same thought, then scurried around in front of him and stood at attention.

"I'm Sora!"

"Donald!"

"Goofy!"

They introduced themselves one after another, and Sora stretched out his arm to shake hands. But he'd reached toward Auron's paralyzed left arm. "…Oh."

Seeing Sora awkwardly stuck there, Auron let out a tiny chuckle. "We must have been fated to meet. Maybe you need a guardian."

"Guardian? Thanks, but…pretty sure we'll be fine." Sora withdrew his hand and rubbed the back of his head, grinning.

"Mm-hmm…" Auron laughed a bit more noticeably this time. "Anyway, let's move."

"Right!" They plunged ahead again.

Meanwhile, up above, bright sunlight filled the Coliseum. There were no games now, and someone from the organization crept through the quiet arena.

Demyx hadn't been able to use his power in those caverns, as if the place was under some kind of curse. Actually, come to think of it, before he came to this world Xigbar had been going on about some kind of talisman. The Olympus Stone—that was it.

"I dunno. I'm just not cut out for this kinda work— *Augh!*" Suddenly, a stout little man with goat horns on his head was standing in front of him.

"What're you doin' here?" demanded the satyr.

"Uh, well, y'know…" Caught out, Demyx scratched his head.

"You here for the games?"

"Huh? Er..."

"Name's Phil. And you are?"

"Um...leaving!"

Demyx dashed for the stone building that served as a prep room for the contestants.

"Hey! Hold it right there!" Phil started in pursuit but found himself beset by a ring of Nobodies. "What d'you think you're doin'?!"

Demyx ran inside as Phil shouted after him.

"The gate!" Donald called and ran ahead to it with the party close on his tail. "Uh-oh... It won't move."

He shoved the door with all his might, to no avail.

"Here goes!" Goofy added his own strength, but the door still didn't budge. Apparently it was not just closed, but locked. There was a sizable keyhole in the middle of it.

"Looks like we're stuck." Goofy looked back at Sora mournfully.

But Sora's Keyblade gleamed. "Oh!" He held it up.

"Can you open it with that?" Auron asked, watching their efforts.

"Yeah. I think so."

But the moment Sora spoke, a dreadful growl sounded from behind them, accompanied by an even more dreadful stench.

"*Wak?!*" Donald started at the sight of the source. It was the giant three-headed guard dog of the Underworld—Cerberus.

Auron calmly faced the beast with his sword ready. "Go!" he shouted to the others, and leaped into action.

Sora nodded and raised the Keyblade toward the keyhole. The weapon glowed and unlocked the gate.

"C'mon!" Donald cried, and shoved the door open.

"Auron?!" Goofy called.

The warrior was busy doing battle with Cerberus. "Just go!"

"We can't leave you behind!" Sora charged at Cerberus and leaped into the air, slashing at one of its eyes. The giant monster dog roared.

"*Tch*," Auron hissed in frustration and charged from the other direction.

Sora and Auron both launched themselves up to attack Cerberus's two uninjured faces.

"Let's get out of here, Sora!"

"Right!"

Auron dashed toward the door with Sora at his heels. Behind them, the wounded Cerberus crept closer.

"Hurry, Sora!" shouted Donald.

They heaved the door shut in Cerberus's faces.

Sora stuck his tongue out at the closed door and grinned. "So there!"

"Huh?" Donald looked this way and that. "Where's Auron?"

Goofy scanned the cavern, too. Auron should have made it through the door with them—but he was nowhere to be seen.

"He's gone…?" Sora searched the premises. No Auron. "Aw… Well, Auron's pretty strong, though. I bet he can take care of himself. Let's go find Meg! Then we can try again."

Donald and Goofy nodded, and they climbed the stairs up from the gate of the Underworld to the shining Coliseum.

Beyond the door atop the stairs, the great stone Coliseum spread out before them.

"Gee, this sure is something else…" Donald sighed, gazing up at the towering walls.

"I wonder where Meg is?" Goofy started toward the center of the arena.

"I wanna see the hero!" Sora ran ahead. The two figures standing in the arena, one big and one small, seemed to be involved in a serious discussion.

"C'mon, champ…"

"Um, 'scuse us…" Goofy quietly spoke up.

"Be right back!" The smaller one went trotting right past the trio.

"Gawrsh, I wonder what's going on?" Goofy mused aloud, just a bit nervous.

"Hey there. Who are you…?" Somewhat at a loss, the taller one looked down at the newcomers.

"I'm Sora!"

"Donald here!"

"And Goofy!"

The tall person smiled at their cheerful introductions. "I'm Hercules."

"So, you're the hero?" Goofy asked.

"Well… Yeah, I guess I am." Hercules laughed bashfully. He wore brown armor over his daunting physique, his blue eyes and white teeth flashing. He gave off an imposing aura, every inch the hero.

Sora stared up at him in awe. "So, we're looking for this lady called Megara…"

"You're looking for Meg?"

"Yeah." The boy nodded.

"Oh, then…" Hercules turned, but just then, someone appeared out of a dark mist.

"Hades!" cried Sora, taking a stance with his Keyblade.

"What's wrong, your hero-ness? Feeling under the weather?" Hades said to Hercules, blatantly ignoring the trio. "I thought staying in perfect shape was part of the job description."

"Hades, we gotta talk!" Sora insisted, but the Lord of the Dead continued to act as if he didn't exist.

"I came to share a little rumor," Hades went on. "Seems your darling Nutmeg went and got herself lost in the Underworld."

"You mean you kidnapped her!" Hercules glared at him.

"Eh, why get caught up in the details?"

Hercules whistled and a winged horse swooped down into the arena.

"Where d'you think you're taking off to? You've got a very

important match today…against the bloodthirsty Hydra!" Hades gave him a wicked grin. "I mean, if you don't stick around to fight it, who knows what kind of accidents might happen?"

"Not exactly accidents when you're the one causing them," Sora interjected.

"Like I said, details."

Hercules clenched his fists. "You're nothing but a coward!"

"Oh well. We can't all be heroes." Hades snickered and snapped his fingers, taunting the hero, then vanished.

Hercules groaned in frustration and hit his fists against his thighs.

"We can handle it!" Sora told him, absolutely confident.

"But… Are you sure? You kids don't really look all that tough."

"We're sure!" Donald pounded his chest boastfully.

"Besides, we were just in the Underworld," Goofy added.

Hercules regarded them anew. "You were?"

"Yup." Sora nodded. "Except…we couldn't really fight… Hades said it was something about the Underworld."

Hercules folded his arms in contemplation and then spoke. "There's a stone that guards against the curse of the Underworld—the Olympus Stone. The gods on Mount Olympus use it when they have to go down there. But…it was stolen." He frowned.

"Huh? Who took it?" Sora asked.

"We don't know yet, but Phil said he saw someone fishy."

"Who's Phil?" Donald asked.

Hercules looked in the direction where the small stout person had run off. "I was just talking to him. He went to follow that man—I couldn't stop him."

"What was this fella like?" Goofy asked anxiously.

"Phil said he wore a black cloak with the hood over his face, and he had an entourage of these quick little minions in white."

The trio looked at one another. A black cloak and quick little creatures in white?

The organization!

"Somebody you know?"

"Sounds like he's one of the bad guys we're fighting," Sora said bluntly.

"Really? Well, maybe I should ask you to help Meg, then." Hercules finally seemed to accept that the newcomers were going to save her.

"Say, if we can get back that Olympus Stone, d'you think we could borrow it for a while?" Goofy asked gingerly.

"Sure… After all, you'll never be able to face Hades without it," Hercules told them with a smile.

Sora, Donald, and Goofy all nodded, determined. "Okay. Don't worry, we'll save Meg!" Sora announced.

"I'm counting on it." Hercules shook his hand.

"Let's go after Phil!" Sora said, and they descended back into the gloomy caverns.

And there, at the gate to the Underworld, they found Phil sprawled on the ground.

"Phil!"

"Ugh… Huh? Oof…"

Goofy ran over and helped him up.

"You okay?" Donald anxiously peered at Phil.

"Yeah, more or less… But who are all you people?" Phil glared, apparently taking them for suspicious characters as well.

"I'm Sora, and this is Donald, and that's Goofy! Hercules sent us after you. We're gonna catch the Olympus Stone thief and save Meg!"

Phil skeptically raised his eyebrows. "Really? The champ sent *you*?"

"He sure did!" Donald bragged.

"Anyway, leave the guy in black to us," Sora said.

Phil still appeared uncertain at first, but then he finally seemed to give in. "Okay, then. If the champ said so, guess I gotta believe him… That guy I was following ran straight into the Underworld."

"Thanks!"

The trio headed for the stone door.

* * *

On the other side, they felt weak again—even weaker than before. But the Heartless kept on attacking them.

"This Underworld curse is really getting to me..." Sora sighed, finally finishing off the Heartless in front of him.

"We've gotta get that Olympus Stone back, fast!" Donald clobbered a Heartless with his wand instead of using magic.

"What if we don't find that organization fella before we run into Hades?" Goofy worried.

"Then we'll deal with it somehow!" Sora proclaimed with confidence he had absolutely no reason to feel.

"Hey... It's you!" called a boyish voice.

"Huh?" Sora spun around, and standing there was a man in the organization-issue black cloak, flanked by Nobodies.

Going by the voice, this wasn't the same one they'd spoken to in Hollow Bastion. He didn't give a very threatening impression, and his hair was almost too long to stand up in spikes the way it did.

"Um... Roxas?" Demyx said timidly.

Roxas...? Sora had never heard the name, if the word was even a name. Baffled, he cocked his head. "Excuse me?"

"...Roxas?" the man asked again.

"What's he talking about?" Goofy whispered to Sora, who shook his head.

"Who knows?"

Donald raised one eyebrow. "He's bonkers!"

"Oh well... No use, is it?" Demyx shrugged, plainly ignoring Donald.

"What's no use?" Sora demanded.

But he seemed to ignore that, too. Demyx took out a piece of paper, skimmed it, and then rolled his eyes. "'If the subject fails to respond, use aggression to liberate his true nature'? Boy, did they ever pick the wrong guy for this one..." Distressed, the man scratched his head.

"You're not making any sense!" Sora burst out.

Again, Demyx made no reply, but only held up a round stone that resembled a medal.

It had to be the Olympus Stone, Sora thought.

"He's the thief!" Goofy declared.

Demyx hunched his shoulders as if offended. "Now that's just plain rude!"

In his hand, the Olympus Stone gleamed.

"*Wa-wa-waaak!*" Donald started at the gang of Demyx clones that appeared. But the doubles weren't solid—they were transparent.

"Let's get this party started!" he crowed, and three of the look-alikes started whirling around.

"Donald, Goofy—let's get 'em!" Sora rushed the doubles and brought down the Keyblade. They splashed like liquid and scattered.

"Are these things made of water?!" Sora spluttered, soaked in what used to be his opponents.

"Let's see how they like getting frozen! *Blizzard!*" Donald flung a spell at them. Goofy spun around, whacking them with his shield.

"Aw, man… I *told* them this isn't my kinda job…" Demyx clutched at his head in frustration, watching one after another of his doubles splashing to the ground. Sora took the chance to charge at him, weapon at the ready.

"Eep…" Trembling, Demyx backed away. "Hey, c'mon… Roxas…"

"Look, nobody knows what that means!"

"Well, uh…" Demyx cocked his head to one side and then the other, cracking his neck, and brought his face closer to Sora's. "I'll just say it—Roxas, come back to us!"

"Who in the world is Roxas?!"

At Sora's obvious irritation, Demyx scurried backward and vanished into darkness. In the same moment, the remaining doubles lost their shape, dissolving into ordinary puddles on the ground.

"What a funny fella," Goofy said.

"Yeah..." Sora lowered the Keyblade and stared at the ground.

Roxas... It felt like he'd heard that word, but he couldn't put his finger on where.

And yet he already knew what it meant, or he wouldn't have asked that question—*Who in the world is Roxas?*

It was someone's name. Someone he knew probably. Except he'd never met or heard of anyone called that.

"What's wrong, Sora?" Goofy asked, his expression filled with concern.

"Oh... Nothing." Sora laughed it off. "That guy really was weird!"

Goofy smiled, too, while Donald scrutinized the cavern floor.

"Oh yeah—the Olympus Stone!" Sora ran over to Donald.

"Didn't he take it with him?" Goofy said.

"It's right here!" Donald picked up the shining stone and handed it to Sora.

He held the Olympus Stone aloft, and the light emanating from it surrounded them.

"Gawrsh, did that get rid of the curse?" Goofy wondered as sparkles rained down on them.

"It must've! Let's go—Meg needs our help!"

Donald and Goofy nodded, and the trio ran down farther into the Underworld.

And deep in the darkest pits, they found Megara being held prisoner.

"Meg!" As they dashed toward her, they realized she was chained to a rock.

"Sora—behind you!" she cried.

The trio turned and came face-to-face with Pete.

"*Gah-ha-ha-ha-ha!* Can't fight in the Underworld, can ya? Well, well, isn't this my lucky day!" Pete stalked closer with a swarm of Heartless in tow.

Sora grinned and readied the Keyblade. "Not that lucky!"

"Chaaarge!" Pete commanded, pointing at the trio.

"You want a fight? You'll get one!" Sora and Goofy took on the horde, while Donald stayed behind to work on freeing Meg.

"Ha! Hya! Take that!" Sora cut down Heartless after Heartless and soon had a path straight to Pete.

"Hey—weren't you supposed to be all weak and wimpy down here?" Pete complained.

"Sorry to get your hopes up!"

At Sora's self-assured reply, Pete broke out in a cold sweat and began to back away. "Eh, this place is a dump anyway. I'll get you twerps next time!"

With that parting shot, he turned tail and ran.

"Hey! You're not getting away!" Sora tried to chase him, but yet another enemy rose up in his path in a billow of smoke. "Hades!"

"Hmm, would you look at that? Buncha tough guys now, huh?" Hades sneered.

Suddenly a bright voice echoed through the dungeons. "Sorry I'm late!"

The one making his gallant entrance was Hercules, along with his winged horse Pegasus.

"Oh, at last, our hero. One little problem, though—down here you're a zero!"

"You're about to find out how wrong you are!" Hercules charged him at full speed, sword in hand, and attacked.

"Wh-what gives?!" Hades yelped.

"Whoa!" The battle ended as quickly as Sora's exclamation, and Hades collapsed to his knees.

"All right, you win—at annoying me!" Hades roared, and blue-white light spouted from under his feet, swallowing him up.

Hercules turned to the trio with a grin. "So, what do you think? Was that heroic?"

"It was amazing!" Donald hopped in delight.

Megara, finally out of her shackles, flew into Hercules's arms.

"Gee, it feels like we didn't even help that much," Sora mumbled, a tiny pout twisting his mouth.

That moment, the Olympus Stone gleamed and floated into the air, where its light became a keyhole.

"Another gate's open...!" Sora lifted the Keyblade and shot a bright beam at the keyhole, and they heard it unlock.

After the light dissipated, the air in the Underworld returned to its usual gloomy state, and the Olympus Stone, as if having finished its work for the day, tumbled to the ground.

"Here, you'd better take this back." Sora picked it up and handed it to Hercules. "Thanks."

"But who are you three?" Hercules wondered.

"We're heroes!" replied Donald.

Meg smiled at them. "Sure looks that way to me."

"Okay, sure," Hercules said. "Junior heroes."

The trio exchanged glances and grinned, too.

"Well, time for us to go," Sora told Hercules, and then they set off on their journey to another world.

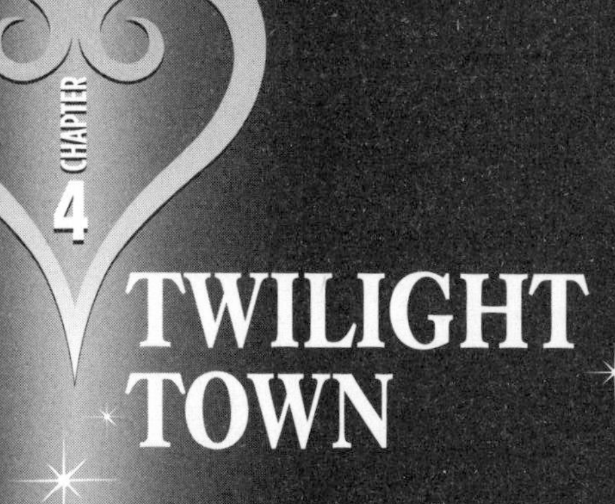

CHAPTER 4
TWILIGHT TOWN

THE GUMMI SHIP ZOOMED THROUGH THE OCEAN BETWEEN. "It's over there this time!" Donald called, peering out the ship's window. They could just see a planet in the distance.

"Say, isn't that Agrabah?" Goofy remarked as he tried to discern it. The desert and palace looked familiar.

"I wonder how Aladdin and Jasmine are doing," Sora said, also casual, as he looked down at the desert world. The Gummi Ship slowly descended to Agrabah.

This place was called the Corridors of Darkness. Stairs and more stairs and pitch-black gloom.

It was connected to all the different worlds...and closed off from them.

Riku walked and walked.

"Help! Please!"

At the shriek from behind, Riku whirled around. It was the second time he'd mistaken that voice for someone else's. "Naminé..."

She flung herself at his back and clung to him. He pulled away for a moment as he moved to face her and gently rested his hands on her shoulders.

She bowed her head for a moment, then raised her eyes to meet his. "Please, Riku—you have to help Axel."

"What happened?"

Naminé's clear, bright blue eyes reminded Riku of *her*...of Kairi.

"The organization is after him." She hung her head again. "He made sure I could get away."

Pursued by the organization—he had expected that, more or less. If he'd been branded a traitor, they weren't going to let him off lightly.

"I can't do anything to help him," Riku said.

"Why not?"

He didn't have a good answer for her.

Why couldn't he help Axel?

If he decided to, he ought to be able to do something…but what good could it do to help a Nobody?

"Is it because Axel's a Nobody? If so, then why were you willing to help me? Because I'm Kairi's Nobody? Because if I'm gone, Kairi will be incomplete?"

"Naminé…"

She was facing downward, her shoulders shaking. He drew her close and held her.

"Axel's heart is hurting," she said.

"I thought Nobodies didn't have hearts." As soon as Riku said it, he doubted his own words.

Did Nobodies really lack hearts? What about Naminé? And Roxas?

As DiZ had told him, those two had both come into being in a special way. Did that mean that they were different?

The members of the organization were also unique among Nobodies—that was obvious. But was that all there was to it?

"Axel's heart says he's lonely."

"How?"

"I don't know." Naminé shook her head. "I don't understand it, either."

Maybe he needed to have another talk with Axel. Riku let out a small sigh and bent down to look Naminé in the eye. "Who's after Axel?"

"One of the men from the organization… He was listening to us." She picked her words carefully.

"What were you talking about?"

"About…Kairi." She said the name softly but clearly.

Riku's shoulders tensed slightly.

"I've wanted to meet her. I thought that I had to, and I asked Axel to take me to her. But…the man from the organization heard me, and he tried to capture me. Axel held him off so I could escape." The story poured out of her, and then she raised her head, realizing something. "…Is Kairi in danger?"

Riku nodded. "We won't let the organization take her. Besides, Axel told you to run, didn't he? He'll be fine. If nothing else, he's fast."

He gave her a hint of a smile, and she returned it, just a bit, as if he really had managed to reassure her.

His breathing was ragged. *I've never had to run like this before,* Axel thought.

"...Ugh." He pushed back his hair and looked at the moon that hung in the unchanging night sky. The neon lights stung his eyes, but the huge bright moon shone through even their blinding glare.

The moon was a heart. The very thing he could never have.

In the end, he hadn't been able to find anywhere to go. So here he was, back in this city of glowing skyscrapers.

If I'm trying to get away from Saïx—from the organization itself—what am I doing here?

The truth struck home—Nobodies had no place where they belonged.

"Now what do I do...?" he muttered, his face still upturned to the distant moon.

A heart. Maybe the answer was closer than he thought.

Suddenly he felt something brush his leg. "Wh—whoa!" Axel jumped.

It was a big yellow dog.

"Hey, what're you doing here?"

The dog looked up at him, tail wagging wildly.

"Are you all alone?"

As if in reply, the dog made a single tiny bark.

"Look, I don't have time to play." Axel gave it a pat on the head and began walking away between the buildings.

There was somewhere he had to go.

Naminé's wish was to meet Kairi. He didn't know what would happen if they did meet. But something would happen—that much was certain.

Sora and Kairi. Roxas and Naminé.

If Naminé got to meet Kairi, maybe something would happen to Sora—to Roxas.

He wanted to bring them together.

"Hey, don't follow me, okay?" He turned and shook a warning finger in front of the dog's nose.

It barked again. The animal almost seemed to understand him.

He'd never had a conversation like this with a dog before—or anything, for that matter.

Axel cocked his head, and the dog copied him.

"Look, I gotta go." Axel opened up a dark rift in space and plunged into the blackness. The dog tilted its head again and plopped down in front of the closing portal as if to wait for him.

All of it disgusted him. Saïx looked up at the skyscrapers, tracking Axel's presence.

He wanted a heart more than anything. But what could he do to get one?

Here he was, yearning for a heart so badly, while Axel had managed to gain one without doing anything at all.

The blue-haired man had been the very first to join the organization after the founding members. He should have been special. The way number 13—Roxas, wielder of the Keyblade—was special. Axel was not. And yet…

He remembered what the witch Naminé had said. *Axel seemed lonely.*

The man himself had denied it, but she was absolutely right.

Axel *was* lonely. He'd lost Roxas.

Lonely. Didn't that mean he had a heart?

How had he gained one? Why only him? Was it an effect of his contact with the boy, or was there something else at work?

He had no idea…

Saïx's searching gaze fell on a yellow dog, and he paused. The dog turned to him with a full-throated bark.

He scowled, crinkling the scarred skin between his eyebrows, and lifted his hand to open a Corridor of Darkness behind the dog.

If something was in his way, he would just get rid of it.

The dog checked over its shoulder and, for some reason, began excitedly wagging its tail, then bounded right into the darkness.

"...Hmm?"

He thought he could see a person there in the corridors. Saïx narrowed his eyes. No, he was sure. He stepped slowly into the portal himself.

The waves lapped against the shores of Destiny Islands with their constant soft swish.

Kairi stood on the sand, watching the sun sink below the horizon.

"Maybe waiting isn't good enough...," she murmured.

"Exactly!" another voice responded, almost before she'd finished the sentence, and Kairi whirled around.

A short distance away, there was a red-haired man in a black cloak.

"If you have a dream, don't just wait. Act. One of life's little rules. Got it memorized?"

Kairi withdrew a step as Axel spoke. It was bizarre, inexplicable—but for some reason she was terrified. "Who are you?"

He shrugged. "I'm Axel. And I happen to be an acquaintance of Sora's."

"Sora...?" Kairi echoed.

Sora—the name of her dear friend.

"Why don't we go see him?" Axel said.

She stared fixedly at his outstretched hand. If she went with this person, this Axel...she would get to see Sora?

"We've got something in common, Kairi. You and I both miss someone we care about. Feels like we're already friends, you know?"

She didn't move a muscle.

* * *

Up ahead in the corridors, Riku and Naminé could see a brilliant light.

"Is that...Destiny Islands?" asked Naminé, squinting. She looked up at Riku.

He didn't reply, his face shadowed under his hood, and kept his attention on the brightness.

The light grew bit by bit, until they could catch glimpses of fine sand and blue water.

Naminé called to the person she could see beyond the portal. "...Axel?"

"Looks like we had the same idea," Riku said, a little relieved.

Naminé halted. "Then...is she there? ...Kairi?"

A girl with red hair was glaring at Axel.

"Hmm... We don't know if he's our friend or not. It's the same for Kairi," Riku said with a faint smile.

"Riku, let's go."

"Right." He nodded—and just then, a yellow dog came bounding up to them. "Pluto?!"

This was definitely him—King Mickey's dog. Pluto raced in ecstatic circles around them.

"Where have you been, boy?" Riku reached out to pet him, but Pluto turned around and growled at something behind them.

"So we meet again, Naminé."

What set Pluto on edge was someone from the organization—Saïx. Before the boy knew it, Soul Eater was in his hand.

"Riku, is it?"

"My name doesn't matter," Riku hissed.

"And through there is Destiny Islands, I suppose—and Axel, too. Well, well." Saïx raised one hand, and a sudden swarm of Nobodies began to wriggle toward the brightness.

"I don't think so!" Riku planted himself squarely in their path.

"What's the matter? Will it hurt to see your island home corrupted?" Saïx taunted. "Even though you once did it yourself?"

A small gasp escaped from Riku.

Yes—his islands had fallen into the darkness once. He'd thought he would never be able to go home again. He wouldn't let anyone spoil that home now.

"Pluto! Go on!" Riku called, and Pluto replied with a deep bark before leaping into the light.

"Exactly what do you think that dog's going to do about it?" Saïx inquired.

"I don't owe you any answers," Riku spat, and dealt Saïx a blow from Soul Eater that sent him sprawling.

The only noise between Axel and Kairi was the peaceful rush of the waves—the sound of Destiny Islands.

A dog's bark shattered the stillness.

"Gah! You again?!" Axel turned to see the same dog he'd met in the city, tail as excited as ever.

Pluto trotted over to Kairi and woofed three times. Suddenly, as if they'd followed him, a ring of Nobodies encircled Kairi.

"Aw, really? You had to bring along these things…?" Axel muttered, arming himself with his chakrams.

Taking out his fellow Nobodies would be unpleasant, but he couldn't let Kairi get hurt.

The girl tried to back away as they closed in on her.

Out of nowhere, a rift opened behind Kairi.

"Huh?" Axel paused.

Pluto raced to the portal and jumped through.

"Hey—wait a minute…"

Kairi glanced back at Axel and then, with no more hesitation, followed Pluto into the darkness.

As if that had been its intention, the portal dissipated, and she was gone.

"What's going on...?" Axel muttered. He hurled his chakrams, and the Nobodies dissolved to nothing.

"Now where'd you go, Kairi?"

He let out a deep sigh and created his own gateway on the beach, then let it swallow him.

The dark portal to Destiny Islands closed. Saïx seemed unaware that Pluto was no ordinary dog—he belonged to King Mickey.

After Riku's devastating blow, Saïx got slowly to his feet. "Nothing less from the great Ansem—that's what I should say, isn't it? Or maybe—"

"You don't know what you're talking about! I'm protecting those islands!" Riku rushed into range, but this time the Claymore, Saïx's sword, was there to block Soul Eater.

"How do you expect to protect anything when you've cloaked yourself in darkness? You sold your soul for power. Was it worth it?"

"Shut up." Soul Eater pushed back the Claymore with a terrific clang.

"Riku! No!" Naminé screamed, running in front of Saïx to stand in the way. "Don't let the darkness control your heart. You've beaten it back before. You made it your strength, remember? You can't let him trick you!"

"You have no part in this!" Saïx slapped her across the face, hard enough to throw her to the ground.

"I feel bad for you, too," she told him.

"What are you talking about?" Saïx towered over Naminé.

"You haven't even noticed yet...that you have a heart."

Several Nobodies emerged from a rift out of the corridors.

"A heart? *I* have a heart? No one wants your nonsense!" Saïx raised his sword over Naminé—but Riku was there with Soul Eater to intercept the blow.

"*Hmph.* I don't have time for these games." Darkness welled from a rift behind Saïx. "Run along and help your dear hero."

With that, he disappeared.

"Are you all right?" Riku helped Naminé to her feet.

"Now I understand...," she murmured.

"Naminé...? You understand what?"

She was silent for a moment and quietly shook her head as she stood. "It's nothing. We have to find Kairi."

"Right..." Riku nodded and found himself staring at his hands.

I sold my soul for power...

Could such power be used for good?

"It sure would be quiet without the Genie," Goofy remarked.

After landing in Agrabah, they'd found Jafar at large, when he should have been trapped in his lamp, and defeated him again. The lamp had unlocked another gate, and they were back on the Gummi Ship.

"It's weird that Jafar was out causing trouble, though," Sora said.

"Yeah! After we already beat him and everything!" Donald complained.

"Gawrsh, I wonder if there's something funny goin' on with all the worlds?" Catching on to their worries, Goofy cocked his head.

Agrabah had been teeming with Heartless, and Jafar had somehow escaped to wreak havoc. There was definitely something weird happening.

"Hey!"

"What, Donald?"

Donald was watching the Ocean Between from the window again, and Sora went to join him.

"A new planet!" Donald indicated something far away.

"Where?"

"Right there!"

Straining his eyes, Sora could just make out a world shrouded in mist.

"But there's one over that way, too," Goofy said, pointing toward something in the distance beyond Hollow Bastion.

"Isn't that…Twilight Town?" Sora spotted a train and a clock tower. He pressed himself up against the window. "I want to go to that one."

"This one is closer!" Donald complained, looking to the other side and stomping his feet.

"I want to go *there*."

While Sora's nose pressed against the glass, Donald and Goofy exchanged glances. He seemed a little different from usual—and it was unsettling somehow.

"I want to see Hayner and the other kids," Sora insisted.

"Oh, fine." Donald didn't sound very happy about it.

Sora immediately whirled around and hugged him. "Thanks, Donald!"

"Wak!"

The Gummi Ship changed direction and sped on toward Twilight Town.

Something warm and wet was touching her cheek. *What is that…?*

Kairi slowly returned to consciousness and found that it was a dog's big pink tongue.

"Hey, that tickles!" She grinned at Pluto.

"You okay?" someone asked.

Kairi bolted upright. "I…huh…?"

Pluto wasn't the only one with her. There were two boys and a girl, all regarding her with worry.

"A hole opened up in the wall, and you and that dog came flying out. Nearly gave us all heart attacks!" said a heavyset boy, sounding a bit relieved.

"I'm Kairi." Still sitting on the floor, she observed the trio. "What are your names?"

"Hayner," said the boy with smartly styled hair.

The heavyset boy and the girl followed suit.

"I'm Pence."

"And I'm Olette."

"Hey...," Kairi said. "Any chance you know a boy named Sora?"

Hearing that name, the three looked at one another.

The sunset in Twilight Town was as beautiful as ever.

"Let's go see Hayner and Pence and Olette!" Sora sprinted through the town as though he'd visited dozens of times—even though he'd only been once before.

"Hey, Sora—don't run like that!" Donald scurried after him and collided with him full force when Sora stopped in his tracks. "*Wak!* Don't stop like that, either!"

"A skateboard!" Sora hopped onto the board lying in the street.

"Uh, S-Sora?"

"Sora...?"

The other two stood there confused as Sora skated in circles around them, then popped the board into the air.

"Wowee!" Goofy cheered, and Donald nudged him in the ribs.

"Hey, have you ever seen him skate like that before?"

"Gee, I guess not..."

While they murmured to each other, Sora performed an aerial grab, clearly enjoying his newfound skills.

Just as he executed an extra-high jump, a boy in a blue coat came running.

"Help! At the sandlot—it's Seifer! Please, somebody help!" Vivi tottered by, hurrying toward the common.

"Sounds like we should check it out!" Sora took off on the skateboard.

"*Quack!*"

"Sora, wait up!"

Donald and Goofy had to chase after him again.

"If you just hang around here a bit, I'm sure you'll get to see Sora," Pence told Kairi.

"He said he'd be coming back," Hayner added hopefully.

"Okay!" Kairi nodded happily, and beside her, Pluto barked with contentment.

"What took you so long, Kairi?"

Everyone rose to their feet at the new voice.

A dark hole in the wall had appeared, the same as when Kairi had arrived, and the one who had emerged this time was Axel.

"Somehow I had a feeling you'd end up here." He moved toward Kairi with a smirk.

"Hey—!" Hayner charged low in an attempt to head-butt Axel, but Axel smoothly dodged it, and Hayner only succeeded in a face-plant. Pence tried the same and likewise ended up on the floor headfirst.

"Anyway, Kairi—that took a lot of guts, jumping right into the darkness like that!" Axel praised her as he grabbed her arm.

"Let me go!"

Apparently, he had no intention of explaining himself as he dragged her back to the portal. Pluto followed them.

"Hey, wait!" Hayner sprang up and tried to pursue them—but they were already gone without a trace.

They followed Vivi to a large open lot. In the middle of it, two boys and a girl were lying in the dirt, with Vivi pacing in distressed circles around them. But he wasn't the only one—the three were also surrounded by strange, wriggling silver creatures. Dusks.

"Guys, we're up!"

At Sora's cue, the trio charged into the swarm.

"Take that!"

Once they'd learned to deal with the bizarre writhing movement, the Dusks weren't actually that difficult to handle.

But there were a lot of them.

"Why are there so many?!" Donald complained.

"Keep at it, Donald!" Sora called, taking down one Dusk after another.

Something about this gave him a strange feeling. Like...he'd fought here before.

And since when did I skateboard...? he had to wonder.

"Finally! We got 'em all!" Sora's Keyblade descended upon the last Dusk.

He heard someone applauding.

"All in a day's work!" He couldn't help striking a pose as he turned. But instead of an awestruck spectator, he found someone from the organization.

"Impressive." Saïx kept on clapping dryly as he strode closer to the trio, who were still poised to fight.

"What do you want?!" Sora demanded.

Saïx paused to speak deliberately. "Have you seen a man named Axel? I believe he's here somewhere..."

"Like we care," Sora snapped.

"You see, Axel's no longer acting in our best interests," the man went on, paying no attention to Sora's hostility.

"Is he in Organization XIII, too?" asked Goofy.

"Yes." He nodded.

"Ooh, infighting!" Donald sounded mildly intrigued.

"Not a very organized organization," Sora added.

"Consider yourself warned." Saïx jabbed a finger at Sora, his voice dangerously quiet. "Axel will stop at nothing to turn you into a Heartless."

"Gee, thanks for looking out for us." Sora stuck out his tongue. "But we can take care of ourselves just fine!"

"That's good to hear. Axel is one thing, but it would just break our hearts if anything were to happen to you."

"Break your hearts? What hearts?" Donald blurted out.

The members of the organization were Nobodies. Which meant they had no hearts.

"True, we don't have hearts. But we remember what it was like. That's what makes us special among Nobodies." Saïx slowly pushed back his hood, showing his blue hair and the cool expression on his handsome face—and his X-shaped scar.

"What's that mean?" asked Sora.

"It means we know the many ways that hearts can be wounded," Saïx replied, and a dark rift in the air opened up behind him. "Sora, you just keep on fighting the Heartless."

Sora ignored him to lean close to Donald and whisper, "Let's jump in after him."

"What for?" Donald whispered back.

"Just an idea! Maybe he'll lead us to Organization XIII's world!"

"Don't be reckless," Saïx chided. "Do you want to end up like Riku?"

Sora raised his head at that. Riku? This guy knew Riku? "Hey—wait!"

Saïx retreated and vanished into the darkness.

"Hold up!" Sora rushed after him, but the portal dissipated in front of his face.

He frowned. "What did he mean, end up like Riku…?"

"Hey, you!" someone else interjected.

"Quack?" Donald turned to find the kids who had been on the ground were now upright and glaring at them.

Sora didn't notice, lost in thought. *"End up like Riku"? What happened to him?*

"I think you better get out of here," one of the boys said viciously. "You've caused enough trouble."

"Fine! We were just leaving!" Donald retorted while Sora was preoccupied. "C'mon, guys."

A bit worried, he patted Sora on the back, urging him to move.

"Hey, hold on a minute!" the boy said.

"What do you want now?!" Donald huffed—but started and gawked at the thing in Seifer's hands.

It was a big trophy set with four different-colored crystals that sparkled in the evening light.

"This goes to the strongest guy in Twilight Town. You should take it."

Sora finally came back to earth and pointed at himself in surprise. "Me...?"

"Yeah."

"Thanks, but...I don't really want it."

Ignoring him, Seifer ran up to Goofy and shoved the trophy into his hands.

"Whoa!" Goofy yelped, not expecting it to be so heavy, and then peered anxiously at Sora.

Apparently satisfied at handing it off, Seifer left the sandlot with the rest of his gang—Vivi and the other two who had been laid out in the dirt, Fuu and Rai.

"What do we do with this thing...?" Sora stared blankly at the trophy.

"Oh, hey! Sora!" a different voice called, and the trio turned toward the source to find Pence.

"Pence? What is it?"

"Do you know a girl named Kairi?"

Hearing that, the three jumped in unison.

"K-Kairi?!" Sora exclaimed. "I sure do!"

"Then you better come to the station! C'mon—we've got something important to tell you!" Pence ran off, and the trio rushed to follow him.

"Kairi...Riku..."

Hearing Sora mumble his friends' names, Donald and Goofy had the same concern.

"Isn't it kinda funny that we're hearin' about both of them all of a sudden?" Goofy said quietly to Donald, running with the trophy under his arm.

Donald nodded. "I wonder if the organization knows about Kairi, too."

That man from the organization had mentioned Riku, and now Pence was talking about Kairi.

What exactly was going on in this sleepy town?

After a short trip through the corridors, they emerged on the beach outside Twilight Town.

"Let me go!" Kairi wrenched herself away, but when Axel let go of her arm, she tumbled to the sandy ground.

"You okay there?"

"Don't touch me!"

A bit chagrined, Axel scratched his head. "Well, look…I, uh—what?! You're still following me?! Oof!"

Just as he began an attempt to explain himself, Pluto pounced from behind and knocked him face-first into the sand.

"Did you come to help me…?" Kairi asked. The dog wagged his tail at her from on top of Axel.

"Get off me already!" Axel shouted as he tried to stand, but this left him open to a slobbery attack from the front. "Ugh! Quit it…!"

Eventually Axel noticed Kairi watching this exchange with mild astonishment and finally shoved Pluto away. Sand covered his black cloak, red hair, and face.

Pluto seemed to lose interest in him and tackled Kairi to lick her instead. "Aw, cut it out!" she giggled.

Axel sighed and tried to brush the sand from his…all over, then stretched his shoulders.

Kairi looked up at him then. "Aren't you…a bad guy?"

"I'm not," Axel replied, completely serious. "But not really a good guy, either."

"This doggy likes you, though," she pointed out.

Axel dropped his gaze, and indeed, Pluto was right there with his tail whipping back and forth.

"Just because dogs like someone doesn't mean they're a good person, y'know. Got it memorized?"

"I don't know what you're trying to say."

"Well…me neither."

He'd dragged Kairi along with him, but he wasn't sure how to explain why. At a loss, he cocked his head. "Uh, I mean… Don't you want to see Sora?"

"Yes!" she replied firmly.

"That might be a problem," said another voice.

They both started, and Saïx emerged from a rent in the space behind Kairi.

"Kairi—!" Axel tried to reach her first, but Saïx snatched her up a fraction of a second earlier.

"Let go—!" Kairi began to scream. It all happened in an instant, and Pluto barked ferociously at Saïx.

"Kairi!" Axel shouted again as the girl struggled against Saïx's hold. He readied his chakrams to hurl at Saïx when a powerful shock wave hit him.

"Traitors like you deserve to lose everything," Saïx said.

Axel grunted and collapsed to his knees in pain from the direct hit. After only one strike, he felt his consciousness fading. His vision was going black. He couldn't even tell whether he saw Saïx disappear with Kairi into the dark portal or whether that was only his own eyes closing.

Is this how I get turned into a Dusk…?

Hayner and Olette huddled together in the station plaza, deep in conversation.

Then Olette noticed Sora and his friends. "Sora…!"

"So you did come back, huh?" Hayner said.

"Pence was just telling us about Kairi… How do you guys know her?" Sora asked.

Hayner and his two friends looked at one another, then down at the reddish stone pavement.

"C'mon, tell me!"

Pence spoke up first. "Kairi came here to Twilight Town."

Goofy was so astounded he nearly dropped the trophy.

"And?" Sora nearly pleaded.

"She said she was looking for you," Olette replied.

"Tell me where she is!" He pressed closer.

The other trio exchanged another glance.

"This guy in a black cloak came and took her away with him…," Hayner explained glumly. "Sorry."

Sora hung his head.

"We're really sorry," repeated Hayner. He bit his lip, genuinely regretful.

That made Sora look up. "It's not your fault," he told them brightly. "C'mon, cheer up!"

"But…" Olette stared at the ground, apparently ready to burst into tears.

"Yeah, guess I've got no room to talk…" Seeing her so upset, Sora mirrored her posture.

Why would the organization take Kairi? And how did they know who Riku was?

There were too many things he didn't understand. It was so frustrating.

"Sora…?" Goofy leaned over, peering anxiously into his brooding face.

"I gotta help Kairi!" Sora burst out.

"A-hyuck?!" Alarmed, this time Goofy actually dropped the trophy, which in turn startled Donald.

"Wak!"

The four crystals in the trophy fell from their settings and rolled away over the paving stones—blue, red, green, and yellow. Sora, Hayner, Pence, and Olette each picked one up.

"This is…," Sora murmured absently, holding up the blue crystal.

"What is it, Sora?"

"Nothing, it's just…" He held the crystal up to the light of the setting sun. It shone, refracting the red beams.

Behind him, Goofy took out the blue crystal from the purse that King Mickey had given them.

Hayner, Pence, and Olette all held their crystals up, too. Five crystals sparkled, two of them blue.

"More treasures for us to share."

Sora spun around, feeling as if he'd heard Hayner's voice somewhere far away. But the Twilight Town kids were quiet, gazing at their crystals in the last of the sunlight.

"Promise?"

Right—he had promised Kairi that he'd find her again.

No…wait. Who had he made that promise to? To split the prize between the four of them… Four?

"Sora!"

"Sora?"

Donald and Goofy were both watching him with worry.

"Huh? What…?" Sora looked around, not quite sure what was going on.

What just happened to me?

He was holding a crystal in his hand. Just a pretty little stone he'd never seen before… As he examined it more closely, it began to shine.

Donald backed away. *"Quack!"*

The light from the crystal formed a big keyhole in the air, and Sora thrust the Keyblade toward it. A beam from the weapon met the keyhole, and a lock opened with a click.

"What is that?" Pence stared wide-eyed at the glow dissipating in the air.

"A new road is open," Sora said, inspecting the blue crystal again. "And Kairi and Riku are somewhere along it."

"Then you'd better hurry." Olette smiled at him.

"You'll be back again, right?" Hayner said.

"You bet!" Sora gave them a grin and faced the setting sun once more.

Somehow, this town was always full of mysteries… But he knew he wanted to come back. It was a special place, different from Hollow Bastion or Destiny Islands.

"I'll see you guys later!" Sora waved to Hayner and his friends.

They squinted at the boy backlit by the dazzling sunset.

But it wasn't just Twilight Town itself that was special—Hayner and Pence and Olette were, too. They were different somehow from any other friends Sora knew.

Was it because he'd been sleeping here? Or something else…?

Sora clutched the crystal tightly. *One more treasure to share.*

CHAPTER 5
UNDER ONE SKY...

AS THEY CONTINUED ON THEIR JOURNEY IN THE GUMMI Ship, Sora let out a deep sigh. Donald and Goofy looked at each other. Perched on a seat in the cabin, Sora was hugging his knees miserably.

"Sora?" Donald peered into his face.

He didn't respond.

"Sora!" Donald yelled, louder this time, and he finally raised his head, startled.

"C'mon, keep your chin up!" Donald tried to sound reassuring.

"But the king, and Riku—and now I've lost Kairi again, too...," Sora mumbled, not encouraged at all.

Donald hopped up and down. "Don't be sad!"

"Yeah! You're the key that connects everything, y'know," Goofy added, coming to stand beside him.

Sora only fell deeper into misery, hiding his face in his knees again. "Because it's all my fault."

"Aw, I didn't mean that," Goofy said, putting his hand on Sora's hunched shoulder. "Just do what makes sense to ya, and we're sure to find 'em."

"That's right!" Donald agreed.

"...Yeah. Thanks, guys."

Sora mumbled with no indication he'd actually cheered up. Concerned, Donald and Goofy exchanged glances again.

"I got it! Say, Sora, why don't we go see Leon and the gang?" Goofy suggested.

"Yeah, I wanna see them, too!" Donald hopped, as if literally jumping on the idea.

"But..." Sora hesitated. "We have to find Riku and..."

"Maybe Leon will be able to tell us something by now," Goofy said.

"Okay... Yeah, maybe." Sora released his knees, and a hint of a smile came to his face. "Let's go!"

As if in response, the Gummi Ship accelerated toward Hollow Bastion.

* * *

Pete paced aimlessly around a room deep in the bowels of the Hollow Bastion castle.

"What in the world are you doing?"

"I'm tryin' to help you, Maleficent..." Pete wriggled, fidgeting.

"Hmm. For all your talk, you're hardly much help at all," Maleficent murmured. "That boy, on the other hand..."

"What boy?" Pete had to ask.

"None of your concern." Maleficent's reply was clipped and cold as she remembered the boy she used to talk to in this room. She'd given him power, a room of his own, and the girl, and still the boy had deserted her.

True, Maleficent had been using him... But the fact that he'd left her without the slightest hesitation was a tiny thorn in her heart.

Her slender eyebrows drew downward as she faced Pete again. "Nevertheless—explain to me what is happening."

"Well, see, there's this Organization XIII that keeps gettin' in the way."

"Let those fools play their little game," she said scornfully.

Pete tried to explain. "But—"

With a piercing glare, Maleficent cut him off. "What? Have you nothing but excuses for me?"

"That runt with the Keyblade! He's been a real pain, too..."

"Sora and his little lackeys?"

Pete confirmed, nodding forcefully a few times.

"I see... Very well. I suppose you'd best tell me what's happened during my absence, Pete."

He wasted no time launching into the story of what Sora and his friends had been up to.

All six of the men in black cloaks were together for the first time in a while.

Xemnas quietly opened the discussion. "So, the princess..."

Kairi, one of the princesses, had fallen into the organization's clutches. Their goal was not to open the door to darkness, but the more pieces under their control, the better.

"Did you take care of Axel?" Xigbar asked.

"Most likely," Saïx replied. Technically, he hadn't seen Axel's end. But it was hard to imagine that he had survived.

"Are you certain he's gone?" Xaldin demanded. "He'll be back to cause more trouble if you didn't eliminate him."

Xemnas put a stop to the interrogation. "Leave Axel for the time being."

"What about the Keyblade wielder?" Saïx asked Demyx, hoping to turn the conversation away from himself.

Demyx only scratched his head helplessly and mumbled like a child getting scolded. "Well, I... Um..."

"You failed?" Saïx pressed, while Demyx struggled to find the words.

"I told you—I'm not cut out for that kinda work..."

"Well, you'll have a chance to make up for it later," Xigbar said, sounding as if he could barely contain his glee at the prospect.

"The circumstances are changing every moment," Xemnas told them calmly. "We must move forward with our work in earnest."

The other members watched him closely.

He could hear the sound of the waves...

"Axel!"

Did I turn into a Dusk...?

"Axel!"

Someone was calling his name. He opened his eyes. "...Nami...né?"

"Oh, thank goodness!"

Naminé sat on the sand, cradling his head. The late afternoon sun was blinding, Axel thought, as he took in his surroundings from the ground. This appeared to be the beach outside Twilight Town. Noticing a man in a black cloak standing beside Naminé, he immediately sat up.

"Don't move yet." It was Riku's voice. Reassured, Axel let himself lie back down—then realized that it was Naminé's lap he was resting on and sat up again.

"Axel?" she said, anxiously tilting her head.

"Oh... I, uh..." He tried to come up with an excuse for sitting up when he should rest, but his vision swam, and he had to simply put his head back down. He just couldn't move yet. Using her lap as a pillow, he accepted her kindness with gratitude—and a hint of embarrassment.

"You're not as tough as you seem." Riku laughed softly.

Axel scowled and closed his eyes. "Not everyone in the organization is as strong as Roxas," he mumbled.

Naminé placed a small hand on Axel's forehead, and he couldn't bring himself to brush away the cool, soothing touch.

"That other one, Saïx... He's pretty strong," Riku remarked.

Axel's eyes flew open. "You met him?"

"Yeah." Riku looked out at the horizon. "He took Kairi."

Axel closed his eyes again. Every time he opened them, the lowering sun was bright enough to sting. "I know."

Riku didn't move, still focused on the line between sky and sea.

"I'm sorry," Axel said, leaving his eyes closed.

Then Riku turned to him. "You should thank Naminé. She's the one who saved you from disappearing."

At that, Axel made the effort of lifting his eyelids again. Naminé was silently watching him.

In the past, he had used her for her powers. He'd never imagined those same powers would save him.

"Sorry... Er, I mean, thank you."

He had to close his eyes again against the sound of those words leaving him.

He had never apologized to anyone before. Or thanked anyone, either.

Without a heart, there was never any need.

If he had no heart, did it mean anything to say that he was lonely, or sorry, or grateful?

The words couldn't be heartfelt, when there was no heart to feel them.

That was a painful truth.

But even that word, *painful*—what could it possibly mean for someone with no heart?

"So, what're you going to do now?" he asked Riku.

Riku crouched down near him to ask a question in return. "How can I help Kairi?"

Axel opened his eyes then and slowly propped himself up. "...You'll have to sneak into the castle."

His vision was still unsteady, and he ached all over. But this was no time for a nap on the beach. Naminé watched him with transparent concern.

"How do I get into the castle?" asked Riku, kneeling in the sand with a similar expression.

"No, I'll go." Axel peered under Riku's hood to meet his eyes.

"How's that going to work? Aren't you a fugitive?"

"I'll figure something out. You just hang back and watch. The castle's pretty huge, y'know." The corner of Axel's mouth curled in a smirk. "In the meantime, I'll check on what the organization's up to."

He stood up, although his legs were still wobbly.

"Naminé, we'll make sure you get to meet Kairi," he told her. "You wait in the mansion."

"Really?" She jumped to her feet, and Axel grinned at her.

"Riku, come back to town once in a while. I'll explain to Naminé about the organization." Axel made a slight gesture with his right arm to create a passage behind him. "You two are gonna help Sora," he told them, smiling brightly. "Got it memorized?"

"Didn't you want to make Sora into a Heartless?" Riku asked, on his feet again.

Axel shrugged. "Changed my mind."

"What's that supposed to mean?"

"I don't feel like telling you." Still grinning, Axel sank into the dark portal.

The trio arrived in Hollow Bastion and headed for Merlin's house. Sora still seemed listless.

Then, along the way, a mass of Heartless crossed their path.

"Ack!" As they backpedaled, hoping to find a way around the fight, the Heartless simply ran away.

"Are there more Heartless than before?" Goofy worried.

As he spoke, Nobodies appeared in clusters as if in pursuit of the Heartless and wriggled away, too. Donald gave a dispirited sigh.

"Gawrsh, I wonder if something's goin' on?" Goofy said, looking at Sora.

"Let's go check in with everyone!" Sora urged. The other two nodded, and they jogged through the market and up the stairs to the residential part of town.

Halfway up, Donald paused, suddenly remembering something. "I wonder if that ice cream is ready?"

At the top of the steps was Scrooge, pacing like before with an ice cream bar in his hand.

"Uncle Scrooge!" Donald waddled up to him.

"Well, hullo there, lad. Still doing well?"

"Yep! What about you, Uncle Scrooge?" asked Donald.

"Ach, I was so close to re-creating that flavor..." Scrooge sighed mournfully at the pale-blue ice pop.

"Can I try it?" Sora leaned toward the tempting treat, just like before.

"Well, go right ahead, but..."

The moment Scrooge replied, Sora leaned just a bit more and took a bite.

"It doesn't taste like anything," he mumbled.

The pretty color of the ice cream pop had promised a delicious dessert, but there was no flavor at all.

"I got rid of the bitterness, but..." Scrooge looked disconsolate.

"Gawrsh, if there's no taste at all, it's just ice," Goofy said dolefully.

"Did you forget what it was supposed to taste like?" Donald asked.

"For the life of me I can't quite remember... What was that town where I'd have the stuff...?" Scrooge sank deep into concentration.

"I bet you'll get it right by the next time we stop by!" Sora grinned at him, trying to sound encouraging.

Even a bite of totally flavorless ice cream seemed to have perked him up a bit.

"We can't wait!" Sora added, and Scrooge nodded. He turned to his companions. "C'mon, let's go find Leon and everyone!"

Considerably more cheerful now, he took off up the street.

When they reached the residential district, it was swarming with Heartless—and not only Heartless, but Nobodies too, milling around like the town was theirs.

"What is going on around here?" Sora wondered between swings at Nobodies. How could anyone restore Hollow Bastion like this?

"Sora!"

Hearing his name, he turned to find Yuffie with her giant shuriken.

"So you came back!" She ran to him.

"What happened to this place?" he asked.

"Um, well..." Yuffie hurled her shuriken, cutting down Heartless. "Maybe we shouldn't have opened the castle gates."

"The castle... *That* castle?" The place where they'd battled Maleficent loomed in Sora's mind.

"Yeah. Oh, but we found the computer Ansem was using!"

"That's good news!" Donald said, bludgeoning the enemy with his wand.

"Leon and the gang are going there now. You should go catch up with them."

"Okay!" Sora blasted away a few white creatures as he replied, "I hope we find out about Riku and Kairi..."

"And the king, too!" Goofy added, shoving back a Nobody with his shield.

"Heh. Well, it can't hurt to go see!" Yuffie exclaimed, sounding for all the world like she was enjoying herself. "Leave the town to me, guys!"

The trio bobbed their heads and threaded their way through the throngs of Nobodies and Heartless toward the castle.

In Hollow Bastion, the Heartless and Nobodies weren't just swarming the town—they were crawling all over the path to the castle, too. Finally, the trio reached a small, mercifully empty courtyard.

"Why are there so many?!" Donald fumed, gesticulating with his wand in his usual temper. The Heartless and Nobodies weren't particularly strong, but there certainly were a lot of them.

"This way, Sora," said a soft voice.

They turned to find another friend. "Aerith! You guys found Ansem's computer?"

"Mm-hmm. And the king is very interested in it."

Donald and Goofy both sprang up at that. "The king?!"

"He's with Leon." Aerith smiled as she delivered the good news.

"Hooray!"

"We get to see the king!"

Donald and Goofy hugged and danced in a celebratory circle with their hands joined.

"Um, Aerith... Is Riku with them?" Sora asked timidly. She shook her head. That took the wind from his sails, but he recovered quickly. "Oh well... Maybe the king will know something about him!"

"Maybe!" Aerith said. "Come on—let's go to the study."

They nodded and headed into the castle through a small side entrance, and at the end of the labyrinthine hallways, they found an unassuming door.

"In there." Aerith showed them the entrance, and the trio filed in.

The small, round room was stacked with books and littered with broken glass flasks. The detritus on the big desk suggested that someone had been in the middle of a project there, and beside it, a single portrait hung on the wall.

"Is that...Ansem?" Goofy cocked his head at the painting. The man appeared younger than the Ansem they remembered fighting.

"This must be Ansem's study," Sora murmured.

"There you are," said another voice.

"Leon!" They rushed over to where he leaned against the wall.

"King Mickey's here, too, right?!" Sora blurted out, almost too eagerly.

"You'll see him soon."

Donald stamped his foot. "*How* soon?"

"Here, this'll tide you over." Leon manipulated something on the wall behind him, and without a sound, it opened. "Ansem's computer lab is this way."

At that information, the trio sprinted down the passageway without wasting a moment.

King Mickey wandered along the winding hallways. He wanted to see Sora, Donald, and Goofy, too, but something else weighed more heavily on his mind.

He'd sensed a certain presence here in Hollow Bastion. He was sure of it.

The king lifted his gaze to the broken wall and murmured the name under his breath. "Riku..."

After they'd parted ways in Twilight Town, Riku had disappeared into the Corridors of Darkness, vowing to help Sora. And if Riku was tailing Sora, it wouldn't be strange to run into him here.

But King Mickey had only felt it for a moment, and now it was gone.

If he could, he'd like to see Riku, too... But maybe that was too much to ask right now.

Maybe it was his own fault his friend had taken that form.

King Mickey decided to search the area once more.

Riku moved silently through the castle of Hollow Bastion. He'd spent a good amount of time here before, and although parts of the place were crumbling, it was without a doubt the castle he remembered.

Where every kind word from Maleficent had been an invitation pulling him into the darkness.

Beneath his hood, he lowered his eyes.

Those memories were painful, but it made sense for him to use them now. Since he was going to atone for what he'd done in the past, the ache was ironically comforting.

Besides, Sora and those other two weren't the only ones he'd sensed somewhere in the sprawling town. King Mickey was here, too.

Maybe I've betrayed the king, Riku thought.

Even if I did, my mind's made up. But...back when I decided to leave the island, I knew I'd do whatever it took. And now, I'm doing whatever it takes to help Sora.

Am I just making the same mistakes over and over?

He breathed a tiny sigh and looked up. And then he called the name of the witch who had first tempted him into the darkness.

"Maleficent."

Nothing around him changed. He called out again, louder. "Maleficent!"

As his voice faded, the empty space before him warped, and the witch appeared in a dark swirl.

"Who are you?" Maleficent said icily.

Riku pushed back his hood. "I've come here to meet with you."

The thin arches of her eyebrows tightened. "Ansem… No—is that Riku?"

He told her the truth with one quiet nod.

At the end of the passageway, there was another room with a big computer and its screen, and opposite the setup was a mysterious red device.

"This is it?" Sora ran to the computer and started tapping at the keyboard. It clicked and whirred softly. "Where's Kairi? And Riku?"

He jabbed harder and waited for the screen to respond, but he couldn't get it to do anything.

"C'mon! Tell us something!" He slammed his hands down on the keyboard in frustration.

Leon walked up behind him and stopped him. "Easy there… You trying to break it?"

"Sorry… I guess I got carried away." Sora turned to Leon, his shoulders slumped.

It was aggravating to be so close to potential information about Kairi and Riku with no idea how to use the enormous machine to access it.

"Sheesh! Just stand back, Sora!" Donald shoved him out of the way and took a crack at it himself.

"You know how to use it, Donald?"

He glanced at Sora sheepishly. "Not really, but…"

"Then what's the point…?" Sora complained.

A moment later, there was an important-sounding beep coming from the computer.

"We did it!" Sora checked the screen—but it still showed nothing. Instead, an ominous voice boomed through the chamber.

"Attention, current user. This is a warning. Further misuse of this terminal will result in immediate defensive action."

"Who's there?" Sora said.

"I am the Master Control Program. I oversee this system."

What was that supposed to mean? Confused, Sora tried asking more questions. "Do you know about Riku or Kairi?"

"Commencing defensive action," the voice announced. *"You are now under arrest."*

"Arrest?!"

A beam of light shot out from the device behind them.

"Run!" Leon shouted, but too late— As the beam struck Sora, Donald, and Goofy, they disappeared.

SPACE PARANOIDS

"SORA!"

The boy woke at the sound of his name. "Donald...?"

"Oh, good!"

Goofy anxiously leaned over him, too.

"Where are we...?" Sora found himself in a strange place bathed in bluish light from a web of glowing lines that appeared to connect somewhere. Sora squinted at it. "What kinda world is this, anyway?"

"You are inside a mainframe system," said an unfamiliar voice.

"A what system?!" the trio echoed, noticing a man perched in front of a screen. He wore a suit covered in radiant blue lines, not unlike the room, and a kind smile.

"For processing data. This is a copy of a large-scale system created by a corporation called ENCOM," he explained freely, and stood up to approach them. "This copy was acquired by another user. The new user updated and customized it, renaming the system Hollow Bastion OS. He used this computer for town administration and private research."

The trio tried to take this in, still totally bewildered. Finally noticing how lost they were, the man scratched his head.

"My name is Tron. I'm a security program," he told them, smiling brightly. "But now I'm in custody, the same as you."

That didn't do much to clear things up.

"Did any of that make sense to you?" Sora whispered to Goofy.

"Uh, maybe we should just introduce ourselves," Goofy said, not too worried about it. Sora and Donald agreed.

"I'm Sora."

"I'm Donald."

"Nice to meetcha, Tron. I'm Goofy."

Tron folded his arms. "With that configuration, I'm guessing you're users?"

"Users?" Sora cocked his head.

Instead of explaining, Tron expressed his concern about something else. "You'd better get out of here quickly. There's no telling what the MCP will do to you."

Sora couldn't follow a thing Tron said. "M-C-P?"

"The Master Control Program. It controls the whole system. If you stay here too long, you'll be de-rezzed."

"De-rezzed?!" Donald jumped.

"How do we get outta here?" Sora asked desperately. De-rezzing sounded pretty bad.

"This terminal should be able to get you back to the user world." Tron pointed to the screen behind him.

"Hooray!" Goofy ran to it.

"But the MCP cut the power about fifty microcycles ago. If we could bring the energy core in the canyon back online, we could power it up again. The problem is…we're stuck in here." Tron indicated the door on one side of the room.

"The door won't open?"

"That's right…"

Sora strode over and held up the Keyblade. The Keyblade shone—and the door opened. "So? How do we get to this energy core thing?" He grinned back at their new friend.

"Remarkable! You seem to have some unique functions," Tron marveled. "I'll go with you to the canyon. You'll need someone who can interface with the energy core, right?"

"Yeah—thanks, Tron!" Sora said.

He replied with a friendly nod.

Outside the cell was a narrow hallway, and Heartless of a kind they'd never seen before seemed to be lying in ambush for them.

"Shucks, they're in here, too?!" Goofy lifted his shield.

"The MCP probably released them to deal with your infiltration," Tron said, completely unruffled.

"Seriously? What a pain!" Weapon raised, Sora charged into the fray and laid the Heartless to waste.

"You three really are something else!" Tron exclaimed, impressed, after the battle had finished.

"Eh, you know."

"But how did the MCP get a hold of you in the first place?" Tron asked as they forged ahead.

"I don't really know… Oh yeah! Tron, do you know anything about Kairi and Riku?" Sora inquired hopefully.

"Kairi and Riku?"

"They're his friends!" Goofy explained.

"No…I don't know," Tron replied. "But maybe you'll find out something if you can access the DTD."

"D-T-D?" Sora echoed again.

"It's a restricted dataspace. I don't know the current password, so I'm locked out. But the keywords that led to the MCP arresting you might be in there, with the sensitive data," Tron explained as they headed down the hallway.

"What's that mean?"

"It means the MCP might have been programmed to automatically arrest someone when they ask about Kairi or Riku."

Sora looked at Donald and Goofy.

"Anyway, we've got to get out of here first," Tron said. "Let's go."

They nodded and continued down the passage.

The gang arrived in a spacious hall with a huge device in the center.

"Is that the energy core?" Sora wondered.

"That's right." Tron began tapping at the keyboard in front of it. The terminal buzzed with a low hum, and the luminous blue of the circuitry brightened into white.

"So, mission accomplished?" Sora said.

"Yes." Tron shyly lowered his head. "Actually… Will you do something for me?"

"Sure!" Sora replied immediately.

"Don't you want to hear what it is first?"

"You helped us, so now it's our turn," Donald said brightly, as if stating the obvious.

"You guys really are users. Your actions are totally illogical."

Again, Sora echoed him. "Illogical?"

Tron had to smile. "Never mind." He shook his head and went to a small terminal in the corner of the room, similar to the one from their cell. Tron set to work at the keyboard, and the screen glowed.

"So, what did you want us to do?"

He turned to them. "Find my user. He'll give you the password to access the DTD."

"Understood!" Donald replied with a salute.

"Um…"

"That's the name my user gave to the dataspace," Tron explained over his shoulder. "Copies of the original programs are stored there, along with any sensitive data."

"The restricted dataspace? So that's where all the secret stuff is?" Goofy asked, watching the program that appeared humanoid, his fingers dancing over the keys.

"Yes. A number of my functions were appropriated the last time I took on the MCP. But if I can get inside the DTD, I can access my original backup program and restore everything. Then I'll be able to get this system back the way it was before the MCP was modified. The way it was supposed to be—a free system for you, the users."

Mystified, Goofy tilted his head. "Gee, Tron…"

"What is it?" He paused to look back.

"Isn't the MCP one o' those programs, too? Do ya know who it was who changed it?"

"Well…"

They waited, but Tron didn't seem to have an answer.

"Actually, I don't know," he admitted, and his shoulders slumped a bit.

The trio exchanged glances at that.

"Okay, we'll just have to find your user and ask him for the password," Sora said. "What's his name?"

"I thought you already knew! It's the user of this system—Ansem the Wise."

"Ansem?!"

The three looked at each other again. They'd never imagined Ansem would have set up a system like this.

"You know, Tron…," Sora started.

"Yes?" The moment Tron replied, the steady bluish lights in the room flashed red. "Looks like the MCP's onto us. I'll keep this terminal up and running. You'd better exit the system now!"

He returned to the screen.

"Um, Tron, Ansem is—"

"We'll get ya the password!" Goofy pulled Sora by the arm.

"Okay. You're good to go. Hurry!" Tron urged, and light beamed from the screen.

The trio disappeared into it, just the same as when they'd come.

Leon stared at the screen after his friends vanished—glared at it, in fact. But if he tried to mess with the computer himself, the same thing would probably happen to him. He couldn't touch it if he wasn't absolutely sure what he was doing.

"Sora…," he muttered, just as a light shone from behind him. "Now what?!"

When he turned, Sora, Donald, and Goofy materialized before his eyes.

"What are you—?"

"We did it!"

Ignoring the stunned Leon, the trio hugged one another with delight.

"Where have you been?" Leon demanded.

They let go and filled Leon in. Not everything Tron had said made sense to them, but they conveyed the most important parts.

When they came to a pause, Leon sighed heavily. "So, basically, we can't get into Ansem's research data unless we know the password... But you already defeated Ansem..."

"Gawrsh, maybe we'll never find the password." Goofy folded his arms, trying to think.

"Which means this is all a wild goose chase," Leon said.

The gang checked to see if anyone had any ideas.

"Maybe we'll find something if we look around Ansem's study...?" Sora thought aloud.

"All right," Leon agreed. "You three search the study. I'll try going through this computer a little more."

The trio agreed and headed back up the passageway.

"D'you suppose DTD stands for anything?" Goofy wondered.

Sora cocked his head. "Data...data...something, something?"

"Anyway, let's see if we can find any clues!" Donald ran into Ansem's study with Sora and Goofy close behind him.

The study, of course, was still a mess.

They opened every single book, rifled through the memos cluttering the desk, left no stone unturned.

"Say, fellas, whatcha up to?"

Donald, startled out of his reverie, sprang up from his position atop the desk—then recognized the voice. "Your Majesty!"

Not quite hidden underneath a black cloak was King Mickey. Goofy promptly swept him up in an embrace, and Donald joined them.

The king laughed as their greeting knocked him over. "Whoa!"

"Where've you been, Your Majesty?!" Donald asked, peering at him closely.

"Shh!" King Mickey held a finger to his lips. "Organization XIII might be listening." He got calmly to his feet, glancing this way and that.

"It's good to see you, Your Majesty!" Sora grinned once Donald and Goofy had managed to calm down.

"Were ya lookin' for something?"

"The password to the DTD."

"DTD?" King Mickey tilted his head thoughtfully. "Now, what's that mean?"

"Um, well..." Sora didn't exactly have an answer.

The newcomer pointed to some scribbles on the wall.

"Huh?" The trio moved for a closer look.

They'd gone through everything in the room, but they had missed the literal writing on the wall—a single phrase scrawled in small letters.

"'Door to Darkness'?" Sora touched the letters with his fingertips. "D...T...D..."

"DTD!" Donald and Goofy both exclaimed.

"The Door to Darkness... That's what Ansem was trying to open," King Mickey explained. They all looked at one another. "But that can only happen with the seven princesses... Remember?"

The trio nodded. With the help of their other foes, Ansem had captured the seven Princesses of Heart in order to open the door.

"So what're you trying to do?" King Mickey asked.

Sora explained the part he could understand. "If we find the password, we'll be able to access Ansem's research data."

The king grinned. "Oh! Then you might be able to find out where he is!"

"Aw, quit joking around," Sora said. "We already beat Ansem! You know that."

Why would the king want to find Ansem so long after they'd defeated him?

King Mickey was rather nonplussed himself. "...Looks like I've got a lot of explaining to do."

"We're listening, Your Majesty!" Donald stayed close to the king as if he couldn't stand to let him out of his sight for a moment.

"But fellas, isn't there someone waiting for your help?"

Sora, Donald, and Goofy looked at one another again.

"Don't worry," the king said with a reassuring smile. "I'll stay right here in town—I'm not going anywhere. If those Heartless attack, I'll stand and fight with everyone else."

"So will we!" Sora smiled back.

"Okay—we'll talk more later."

"That's a promise, right?!" Donald pressed.

"I'll see ya when you get back." The king nodded to them, and the trio returned to the computer lab.

When they arrived, they found Leon glaring morosely at the screen.

"Leon!" Sora ran up to him.

"Did you find out the password?"

"Yup!" Goofy said.

"So you're going in again?"

Sora nodded. "See ya soon!"

Leon tapped a few keys, and the laser beam from the device behind them shone on Sora, Donald, and Goofy.

After a few moments in the dark, a familiar bluish glow illuminated the room around them—apparently the same place they'd first met Tron.

"Where's Tron?" Sora wondered, searching for his friend—and finding him collapsed on the floor. "Tron!"

Sora rushed to him, and he seemed to wake up upon hearing his name.

He rose unsteadily to his feet. "I don't understand. Why are you here...?"

"We came to give you the password!"

Tron rubbed his forehead, sounding upset. "You could have just transmitted the data."

"'Transmit'?" Donald asked, but before Tron could explain, his legs wobbled and nearly buckled under him.

Sora barely managed to catch him. "Hey, are you okay?"

Tron smiled weakly. "I'll be all right…once we access the DTD."

"Well, okay, but…" They regarded him with concern.

"Let's get going." Tron walked—well, staggered—forward, and Sora slipped his shoulder under Tron's arm to help.

"Are you sure you're okay?"

"Yes…"

It was hard to tell under the bluish light, but Tron seemed horribly pale.

"Did the MCP do something to ya?" Goofy asked anxiously.

"…Don't worry." Tron smiled without confirming or denying. "The DTD isn't far. Let's go."

They forged ahead with Tron leaning on Sora. The route to the DTD was teeming with Heartless, but they made it through.

The room containing the restricted dataspace had three big screens.

"Is this the DTD?" Sora said.

"Yes… Now, what's the password?" Tron rested his hands on the keyboard in front of the screens.

"Uh, Belle…Snow White…" Tron typed in the names as Donald gave them.

Goofy continued the list. "Aurora, Alice, Jasmine, Cinderella…" Before he named the last one, he turned to Sora.

"Kairi." Sora pronounced it slowly.

"…Kairi, right?" Tron looked back at Sora for confirmation.

He nodded.

"K-A-I-R-I…" The moment Tron finished typing, the screen began flashing. "It worked!"

He jumped into a victorious pose. The password had granted them access to the DTD. He placed his hand, palm down, on a panel in front of the screen, and his outfit glowed blue white. "All my functions are restored. I'm as good as new!" Tron told them with a grin, and he did look healthier.

"That's great, Tron!" Sora grinned back—but then the buzz of an alarm filled the chamber.

A voice broke into sinister laughter. "*Ha-ha-ha-ha!* Finally, I have full access to the DTD! My takeover of the system is complete. I might have anticipated such a simple password..."

"It stops now, MCP! We won't let you do this!" Tron shouted.

"Hmm, what's this? A self-destruct program for the entire town. Let's see how it performs..."

"No!" Tron's fingers flew across the keyboard.

"You, program—you changed the password!" the MCP bellowed.

Tron ignored it. "That should buy us some time," he told the trio.

"Tell us what's going on!" Sora pleaded.

"The MCP is loading a hostile program into the I/O tower."

"Gawrsh, does that mean Hollow Bastion's gonna be destroyed?"

"*Wak!* What do we do?!"

"We've got to protect the users' town. Let's head to the tower!" Tron said, and the trio agreed.

A broad pillar with red lights zooming along it stretched high into the strange sky.

Sora stared up at it. "So that's the I/O tower...?"

Beside him, Tron strode toward the nearby terminal when they heard a huge rumbling—and something enormous fell from the sky. Two powerful-looking arms protruded from a round body covered in spikes. It could be a Heartless, but Sora figured it was the hostile program meant to destroy the town. It definitely radiated hostility.

"Here it comes!" Sora brandished his Keyblade.

"Your actions are disconcerting, Tron," the voice of the MCP declared from somewhere overhead. "Why do you insist on allying with these selfish users?"

"Because I want to help them." Tron took a step forward. "Something in my code commands me to."

"Really? What sort of code would command that?"

Tron considered the question for a moment before he replied, looking at his new companions. "I don't really know for sure."

"Friends help each other, that's all!" Sora declared. "Uh-oh—look out!"

Just as he spoke, the program fired a laser from its arm.

"Ngh!" Tron evaded it and ran.

"Fire!" Donald cast his magic, while Goofy charged at the program with his shield. There was a *clang!* and the program briefly halted.

"Huh…? It stopped?"

"Don't let your guard down! It just froze!" Tron dashed in under the program and withdrew the small device he'd been carrying to start typing on it. "Sora!" he called.

The device emitted a ray that seemed to damage the program.

"Got it!" Sora lunged and slammed the program with his Keyblade, and in the next moment, light burst from the gaps between its parts, and it fell to inert pieces.

Tron and Sora high-fived. "We did it!"

"That's a load off our minds," Donald added cheerfully.

"All right, I'd better get you users out of here." Tron headed for the terminal off to the side and crouched down at the keyboard. "With my functionality restored from the backup, I think I've got a chance at getting control of the system back from the MCP. I have to get to work fast. It's what my user would want." The keys clicked as he talked.

"What your user—what Ansem would want…," Sora murmured. Donald and Goofy gave him a look.

"Sora…?"

"I know. I'll tell him." Sora nodded. Tron was still facing the screen. "Listen, Tron…"

"Yes?" He stopped and turned to them.

"We didn't get the password from Ansem," Sora told him. "We just happened to find it back in the user world. And one more thing. Ansem—he was our enemy. Well…he still is, I guess."

Tron narrowed his eyes slightly and got to his feet. "The truth is… he's my enemy, too." He sounded determined.

"What do you mean?" Sora asked.

"Ansem built this system by customizing ENCOM's original system for his own use. I was part of that original system, and Ansem modified me, too. That makes him my user."

The trio nodded, following so far.

"But he's also the one who made the MCP the way it is now. The Ansem I knew wouldn't do that. I'm sorry I didn't tell you."

"Okay, but…" Sora cocked his head. "Now I really don't get it."

Ansem had created this system to protect Hollow Bastion, but then he'd altered it? In that case, Sora had no idea what Ansem was trying to do.

"I don't think it's in my programming to understand," Tron admitted. "Users like you will probably be the ones to figure it out. You have the capacity to take illogical routes to arrive at the answers you seek." He shrugged with a shy smile. "You should go now, before the MCP starts acting up again!"

Tron gestured at them to get in front of the screen.

"Any data you need from the DTD can be accessed directly through my user's terminal. I'll keep a dedicated access channel open for you. And since I changed the password, you won't have to worry about the MCP for a while."

"Access…channel?" Sora repeated.

Tron laughed for some reason. "I knew you'd ask. It's important—the link between our worlds. It's how we stay connected."

That made sense—or at least, it felt right. The trio nodded, and finally a device by the screen fired the familiar beam at them.

"Sora—my friends are the new password!" Tron told them as they blurred and pixelated in the transfer.

Tron's friends.

"Does that mean—?"

Tron held a finger to his lips, then grinned. "Don't let the MCP hear it. You'd better go!"

"Thanks, Tron. Take care!" Sora said as they waved to Tron.

"You too. And give my best to the other users!" they heard Tron say as they disappeared from the system.

"All taken care of!" Sora announced eagerly, back in Hollow Bastion's computer lab.

"Look at this." Leon gestured to the screen, as if he'd been waiting to tell them something.

The screen showed little caricatures of Sora, Donald, and Goofy with the caption THANK YOU!

"Hang in there, Tron," Sora said softly, peering at the image.

"So…where do we start?" Leon asked.

"I know—let's access the DTD!" Sora went to the computer and leaned over toward the screen. Behind him, Donald and Goofy scanned the room for something.

"The king's checking the situation in town," Leon said. "Don't worry, he'll be back soon."

"That's good to hear!" Donald smiled, relieved.

"So…how do we use this?" asked Sora.

"Just a second." Leon started typing. "Hey, it's asking for a password." He turned expectantly toward the trio.

"Oh, that's easy." Goofy eagerly shifted closer to the screen. "It's…"

"Sora!" The boy cut in with his own name.

"Sora…?" Leon frowned, dubious, as he typed it in.

"Donald!"

"Goofy!"

The other two completed the list.

The password was "Tron's friends"—which had to mean their names.

"Well, that's...to the point," Leon remarked.

"Did it work?" Sora watched Leon's hands on the keyboard.

"Yeah, we're in. Now I have to go into town and see how things are."

"You're not gonna look at the data?" Sora complained. "It wasn't exactly easy to get!"

"I'm coming right back. Sora, why don't you get started on loading the data and copying it?"

Sora squinted, a little confused by the instructions.

"You just use the keyboard to tell it what to do. It's pretty straightforward." Leon left with a little wave and not a glance behind him.

"...You think you can do it?" Donald said, not looking very confident.

"Maybe, if you're not on my case!" Sora reached for the keyboard, took a deep breath, and tried pressing the biggest button. The screen immediately displayed something else—strings of questions for them. "Whoa... It's doing something!"

"'What would you like to search for?'" Goofy read aloud.

"Riku and Kairi!" Pecking at the keys with his index fingers, Sora input their names.

The monitor showed a progress bar, and then went red, clearly indicating that something was wrong. A voice came from the computer. *"No data."*

"No way..." Sora slumped over in dismay. "Even Ansem's computer doesn't know...?"

I really thought we'd find something about Riku and Kairi in here. He shuffled away from the workstation, and Goofy took his place.

"Whatcha doin'?" asked Donald.

"Well, I thought we could ask the computer about those Nobodies." Frowning in concentration, Goofy punched in the query. This time the screen answered with lines of incomprehensible text.

"What's all that?" Sora muttered from behind Goofy.

"The data is corrupt." The same red light flashed as the computer spoke.

"How about Organization XIII?" Goofy tried again. After a few seconds, it happened again—the lines of text, the alarm, and the computer's inorganic voice announcing, "The data is corrupt."

"Stupid computer!" Sora banged the keyboard with his fists.

"Sora!" Goofy tried to stop him, but Sora kept on hitting, unwilling to be pulled away.

"You're gonna break it!" Donald scolded.

But then an image of a person appeared on the screen. It was an elderly man, his hair and beard pale, and he wore a red scarf over what appeared to be a lab coat.

"Who's that?" Sora asked as they stared at the unfamiliar man.

"Well, I see ya got things working!" a voice exclaimed from behind them.

"Your Majesty!" Donald jumped. The king was back.

"Shh!" King Mickey shushed them with a finger to his lips again. "Good going! This computer should tell us what we need to know."

He came closer to the screen.

"But it just keeps on sayin' the data's all kerskuffled," Goofy said dejectedly, and Donald bobbed his head in agreement.

"All we got is a picture of some guy we don't know," Sora added.

King Mickey peered at the monitor. "Why, that's Ansem!" he exclaimed.

Sora, Donald, and Goofy exchanged confused glances. The man on the screen was someone they'd never seen before. It couldn't possibly be Ansem.

Sora folded his arms. "Come on… Are you trying to pull one over on us?"

"Didja forget what Ansem looked like, Your Majesty?" Goofy wondered, a little worried.

"'Course not! This is Ansem the Wise!" King Mickey said, still focused on the screen.

"Quack?"

"Uh, Your Majesty, would you come over here a minute?" Sora

grabbed the king by the arm and took him back to Ansem's study. Donald and Goofy followed them.

The painting in the study was a portrait of Ansem. That should remind King Mickey what he looked like, Sora thought. He stopped in front of the painting. "See, *this* is Ansem. You know, the guy we all worked really hard to defeat?"

"Oh, that's right—I never finished explaining."

"*Wak?*" Donald peered nervously at the king.

"The man in that picture is definitely the one who tried to take over Kingdom Hearts—the one you fellas defeated. But what you actually fought was his Heartless. He wasn't really Ansem—he just went around telling everyone he was."

At this revelation from King Mickey, the trio could only stare up at the portrait.

"Wait... *Whaaaaat?!*" they shouted in unison, startling the king.

"We went through all that trouble fighting an impostor?!" Crestfallen, Sora hung his head.

"Yup, a fake—but he still had to be stopped," King Mickey said, trying to be supportive.

"Boy, this is kinda depressing," Donald grumbled at the portrait.

Goofy was the only one who seemed confused rather than discouraged. "Gee... Then, if he was a fake, what happened to the real one? That Ansem the Wise fella?"

"That's just what I'm tryin' to find out," King Mickey replied. "Ansem the Wise should know all about Organization XIII's plans and what's been happening to the worlds. I'm pretty sure he can help us out. I came close to finding him once..."

Goofy still looked bewildered.

"So there's more?" Sora said. "I'm lost enough as it is!"

"Uh, so... Let's see...," Goofy started, trying to sort it out. "Somebody who wasn't really Ansem became a Heartless?"

The king nodded.

"So, does that mean a Nobody got created when that happened?" Goofy observed the painting again.

"That's right! And that Nobody's the leader of the organization."

"Whaaat?!" the trio shouted, flabbergasted again.

"I know I've met that fake Ansem before...," King Mickey went on, looking up at the portrait. "And I've seen the leader of Organization XIII, too. Kinda felt like being around the same fella."

"So where did you meet this guy?" Sora asked.

"I can't remember." King Mickey crossed his arms, looking frustrated. "But Ansem the Wise—the real Ansem—he must know who the impostor really is. That's why I've gotta find him."

Sora furiously glared at the painting.

If it weren't for this fake Ansem, none of this would have happened. Riku and Kairi would be safe.

He's the one who started all this. Sora hated the man so much he could hardly think.

I hate him. I really do.

He'd never loathed anyone like this before.

No matter how angry or sad anyone had made him in the past... hating someone like this had been unthinkable until now.

He thought of Riku and Kairi. Where were they now? What were they doing?

Then, suddenly remembering, he turned to King Mickey. "Oh, right! Your Majesty, do you know where Riku is?"

The king jumped a bit, as if the question caught him by surprise, and kept his back to Sora as he replied, "He's... I'm sorry. I can't help."

Sora walked around to look King Mickey in the eye. "Really? You don't know? Are you sure?"

But the king avoided him and turned away again. "I'm sorry, Sora."

The boy bit back more complaints and asked a different question. "What about Kairi? Organization XIII might've kidnapped her."

This time the king spun around to face him. "Oh no…!"

Then he gazed up at the painting again, thinking, and addressed each of them.

"Sora, Donald, Goofy… I was thinkin' I'd go get help from Ansem the Wise. But— Now I know I forgot something really important. Helping others ought to come before asking others for help. I shoulda kept that in mind." Slowly, King Mickey turned to look at them. "We're here safe and sound and free to choose what we'll do. So there's no reason we shouldn't choose to help our friends."

Sora and the other two nodded solemnly.

"Let's look for Riku and Kairi together," the king said, but before anyone could respond there was a huge rumble, and the room shook.

"*Wak?!*" Donald blurted out.

"Outside!" Sora turned to the door.

"Sounds like we gotta start by helpin' out our friends here!" King Mickey's expression was grim as he dashed to the exit.

"Donald, Goofy—let's go!" Sora said, and they nodded at him. The three followed King Mickey out of the castle.

They were on their way to do the most important thing—to help their friends.